Disclaimer

This is a fictional work in an imaginary country. Any perceived resemblance to people is purely coincidental and the author apologizes in advance.

Foreword

The sacrifices made by those who choose to become doctors are immense. While their contempories were moving ahead with their lives, those who chose medicine spent endless hours of learning, and forefeited potential earning opportunities and in fact paid hefty tution fees in many instances, to pursue their dream.

Those among the doctors who chose to become surgeons shed sweat, tears and blood to reach their goal. If one thought that this would be the end of their suffering, one is mistaken. By becoming surgeons these doctors were entering a world of intrigue, manipulation and bullying.

This exciting novel is about a paintedsurgeon's fight back from a tight corner. Did he succeed? Please read till the end. It will move you.

My sincere thanks to my dear wife Dr. Mythily Ramanathan who has stood by me during the ups and downs of life. I also thank my aunt Parvathy Nagasundaram who taught me English from a very early age, giving me confidence to rub shoulders with native speakers.

Thank you

Ezhuth Aani
Jamaica
New York,
USA
Nov 11 2021

Chapter 1

There was pin drop silence in the room. It was an old building which had probably been a home at some point in its history. Now it was being used as an office. The old cottage style brick building would have been a charming place for a home stay or a romantic dinner. The largest room, which was probably the main living area in the original plan, had been converted into a hearing room. The room had high ceiling which made it look even larger than it actually was. The walls had been fitted with polished wooden panels which gave it a formal appearance. It was déjà vu. He had been there several months prior, when a purported "draft report" of an "external review" resulted in some restrictions, though none of the details were discussed. Then his career was placed in a slow cooker, waiting for the next boil. The second hit!

The long rectangular table separated him from his adversaries. Just two of them he had to face on that day. The table occupying most of the length of the room, he was seated at one end and the two people who were going to judge him, at the other end of the room. His lawyer was seated to his right. That made it two of them versus the two judges. The distance was very daunting. It was actually inhibiting good communication. He felt intimidated. It felt like he was in the TV Quiz show "The Chase." Only here the chaser did not have to answer any questions. The odds were totally stacked against him.

It was unbelievable that such a process existed in a free western democratic society. Perhaps this belonged more to the Soviet Union, just before the prisoners were sent to Gulag. Or North Korea, before the dissidents who dared to speak against "Dear Leader" were sentenced to death. Yes, they were contemplating sentencing his career to death. Just two people, a doctor and a lawyer, were going to judge him based on his treatment of one case. And it was not even like he had sexually assaulted a patient, or swindled money from the public. Just one complication this time, and his whole career had been put on a knife's edge. His entire life's work hung in balance. He was waiting to hear the final verdict that would decide whether he could practice medicine, at least in the short term.

The woman who was delivering the verdict tried to show a kind face. It was like rubbing salt to his injury. She was trying to feel good about her treatment of this horrible leper who is the scourge of the society. She was being humane. Even though she was sentencing this man who had had a horrible complication, she was upholding her humanitarian values. Did he even detect a smile on her face? Did that mean they had decided favorably in his case? Or was it his imagination?

He waited with bated breath. His lawyer had told him not to display any emotion. He tried hard to appear calm.

Every passing second was like an eon. They were all standing for the delivery of the judgment. He was feeling a flutter in his heart. His legs were getting weaker by the second. He was feeling dizzy. Was it the standing? Was it the lack of a proper meal for the day? Or was it just anxiety?

"Your license has been suspended" announced the Chairperson. "You may appeal according to the provisions in the law. The suspension comes into immediate effect. You shall not have any patient contact. You will not consult nor operate. Written reasons will be given in due course."

It was a thunderbolt from nowhere. He did not see it coming. He had heard about doctors being suspended. Usually it was for having sexual relationship with a patient or for substance abuse, being drunk at work, or falsifying medical records and such offences that bring into question a doctor's character, and thereby his capacity to act in a position of trust. But He? He did not do anything of that sort.

Just two people had sat in a "committee" and banned him. All the years of hard work, the sweat, tears and blood (yes literally, blood) that he had shed to come to this position. All the exams he failed and passed; all the midnight oil he burnt; all the professors who examined him in the numerous exams thrown in his path. All of that had come to naught. Just two people, a lawyer and a mid level doctor, had constituted this committee and nullified, in a few hours of ritual humiliation, everything that he had achieved. He was a loser. He has lost.

To whom did he lose?

The wily old fox who brought him down to his knees. He was a formidable opponent indeed. Well he had thought the world of this man at one point. It was the fame of this man that made him apply for this job. But now he was on the wrong side of this man. He was at the receiving end of the wrath of this powerful man.

All his life up to that point has now gone up in smoke. They say there will be no smoke without fire when there are complaints about a doctor. But the fire that burnt down his career - no one was willing to see it for what it was though the dense smoke and the choking cough was there for all to see and smell.
No one was seeing the elephant in the room. The Head of the Department had undermined one of the surgeons and brought his own son in his place. But not a

single person raised his voice. There was a climate of fear. No one wanted to be in the bad books of this man.

And he had tried to fight his own battle. Only then did he realize how difficult it was to fight a cartel. Yes it was a surgical mafia. Where ever he turned there was fox and friends. He was alone. And after he was shunted out of his job he found himself outside the fence. Like a rabbit trying to breach the barrier. He was realizing how hard it was to fight someone from outside. He should have fought from inside. He should have fought from within. But then he was afraid to speak. He was too scared to start an open war. He knew his boss was undermining him. But he had no proof. In fact he did not even know that this man had a sinister agenda. That he had a son who was finishing training. That he wanted to hand over his empire to his son.

Otherwise he would not have trusted this man. He would not have trusted that there was justice in the land. He may have quit earlier before things came to this pass. Or he may have fired the first shot.

But being a nobody would anyone have taken him seriously if he had started the war; if he had brought everything to the open?

Should he have flagged the high amputation rates? That would have been against the prevailing culture. He had heard comments such as "It's only a leg" and "Remember that putrid leg? It paid for a few tiles in the swimming pool." Well it was not their leg. And who cared if someone lost a leg? It was not like it was a young amputee who would have carried on from where he left on an artificial limb. These were elderly patients who lost their mobility, and therefore their freedom and independence, and would then be confined to a wheel chair and dumped in a nursing home during the last little period of their lives. Who cared as long as it was not their own leg?

Or should he have spoken out when he watched in abject horror as a carotid stent was being placed in the left internal carotid artery? The filter that was placed above the area of the stent in order to capture any debris or clot and prevent it from going into the brain, had come down thrice to below the lesion in a fully deployed state, and each time was pushed up, that is, crossing the diseased part of the artery six times. Not once. Not twice. But six times!

A filter is like an umbrella with a net, contained in a small hollow wire. It is deployed only after it reaches a suitable area above the site where the stent would be placed. Once it is deployed it should not move at all until after the main procedure is done. Then it is carefully collapsed into a catheter along with any material that it may have collected, intercepting the latter from causing a stroke. For a deployed filter to move up and down like that was something he had never witnessed. Well, not until that time. He cringed. He was too scared to speak out. Everyone else in the room too kept their silence. See no evil. Speak no evil. At least no evil about the big Alpha.

He was too scared to even check if the patient had a stroke. In any case the outcomes don't matter he had been told. It is how you perform your surgery that matters. It was vitai lampada. Play the game. Play according to their rules. That out comes don't matter was not surprising at all. It was who you were and how you played the game that was important. He had once done a clam shell thoracotomy to save the life of a patient who was bleeding rapidly in the left side of the chest. Bleeding so heavily that the entire left side was a white out in the chest X ray and the blood pressure was in the boots. Clam shell thoracotomy is when the chest is opened across in the middle, literally like a clam shell. This was the quickest way to enter the chest he had been taught.

That the patient lived and went home in ten days did not matter. The other doctor criticized him for not doing a sternotomy, where the breast bone is split vertically. That was what the latter had been taught in a training course. So he complained.

The man who saved the patient's life was put through the works, including being drug tested - he had to give the urine sample in front of a woman so that he did not cheat - and nine months of hell and a performance assessment. If the reader thought this was Soviet Union, it certainly was not. In any case the point here is that outcomes did not matter as long as you belong. If you don't belong, there is a problem, with you - God save you.

He thought about the time when he called in the Boss, the big Alpha, for help with a case with a clot in the main artery to the gut, the superior mesenteric artery. The clot had to be removed expeditiously and the circulation restored before the bowel died. He regretted calling for help as the person whom he trusted to have superior experience and skills than him ended up treating the affected artery so roughly that he destroyed the artery. They had to resort to a bypass. The patient died mysteriously within a couple of months, presumably due to the twisting of the bypass.

The see no evil attitude was not confined to the operating room. It continued to the wards too. He could only watch aghast as the Boss examined wounds with his bare hands, without wearing gloves. This was contrary to all the teaching that he had had. Yet when the boss did it, no one dared to challenge him. Such was the fear.

And he had trusted this man. The big boss close to retiring. He thought if I put up with this man for a couple of years he will leave. I should not rock the boat now. I shall inherit it all when he is gone. Little did he know that the boss had other plans. His son was in training. He needed a couple of years before he was ready. So the man he recruited was just a seat warmer. He was keeping the place for the son. Then the father and son shall rule the world. The kingdom will be handed over to the prince in waiting. Then the emperor could retire in triumph, his kingdom intact.

Had he known about this sinister plan he would have left at the earliest sign of trouble. He would not have trusted that justice would prevail and the truth shall come out and set him free. He had wasted a few years of his professional and personal life as a pawn in the big man's game of chess.

He had sacrificed his career so that the son may have his. They should have thanked him. But did they? No! He has been vilified and hounded out. Survival of the fittest. Perhaps he was not fit to be among these wolves. It was law of the jungle.

Kipling had summarized the rules beautifully in his poem about the pack.

"Because of his age and his cunning, because of his gripe and his paw,
In all that the Law leaveth open, the word of your Head Wolf is Law..."

If only the Head Wolf had laid the law firmly in front of him..he would have known his place and gone away. But that would have been wrong timing. The cub had to be ready before the ejection button was pressed.

Was he in denial when he stubbornly stayed on the scene even after his public hospital appointment had been terminated? But how could he have just left the area and fled the scene. He had built up a practice. He had a patient load in his books. He had won the trust of the referring doctors. And he had his employees to worry about. He had signed up lease for his office, and he had signed up a mortgage for his other office. He had painstakingly developed a vascular ultrasound laboratory. He had put his roots down in the area. He was well known in the community. How could he have walked away from all this?

He was made of sterner stuff. He would stay and fight back. So he thought. But it was like playing a game of chess without your queen, or like playing a card game with all the Aces loaded in the opponent's hand. Truth will prevail, he had thought. Perhaps it will. But not in his life time. Certainly not in his working lifetime.

So he was stuck. A prisoner of circumstances. Stuck in a dying practice. Or rather, a murdered practice. Trying to make ends meet. Trying to pay the rent and the salaries. Trying not to declare bankruptcy. Trying hard not to default on his payments. This couldn't have gone on for long.

But he was hoping that justice would be done. At least someone would hear his plea for fairness. He had complained to everyone, from the bureaucrats to the politicians through to the eminent people in the profession. But no one seemed to be capable of hearing.

Then the final blow. It was only a matter of time before the wrath of the Head Wolf would bear down on him. He had been naive. He should have known.

Chapter 2

"It's nearly done," Beta was in charge of the barbecue. "Let me bank the coal and let the ribs continue in carry over cooking."

There was an assortment of marinated pork chops, ribs of beef and turkey breasts. He had already grilled the asparagus, corn cobs, eggplant, Portobello mushrooms, and halved tomatoes. There were some poached eggs too. It was a complete meal. Call it Atkins or South Beach. Beta knew his cooking, and of late he had started cutting down on the carbs. Everybody who was middle aged did that at the hospital.

His wife had already made a salad using her own imagination. She was good in what she did. His guests had baked a chocolate cake for the occasion. It was a fine celebration.

Beta got rid of his apron, washed his face and hands quickly and joined the group. After the initial formalities the ladies were shooed into the house while the men stayed out. They had said cheers to the happy and prosperous future ahead of them, though the chief guest of honor had only water. He was a teetotaler.

"We need to talk business" said Alpha. "We don't want the ladies in here." Once they were alone they high fived each other.

"Are you sure it went the way we wanted?" asked Beta. He was always cautious. He did not want any unexpected surprises.

"Oh yes. I got confirmation." Alpha bit his tongue as he said that. He did not want to let in Beta on his secrets. After all they had been fierce adversaries for nearly ten years. Things could turn back to the icy past any time. And he did not want Beta to be armed with any knowledge that could jeopardize his own reputation. But Beta understood that his friend was well connected in the high places.

This was their second honey moon. The first time around, they had been friends for nearly a decade and then fell out. Alpha was always the dominant control freak and Beta the submissive partner in the relationship. But when things soured Alpha had made Beta's life a living hell. So much so that Beta had run away to another country for six months. Since that time they had not spoken with each other for nearly ten years. Beta was on the verge of being pushed out of business until he found a brilliant solution. He had played on the one weakness that Alpha had. And that worked like magic. It gave him a lease of at least five more years of practice, after which he could retire comfortably. It also gave him an opening to mend his relationship with Alpha at least on a superficial level. Not as vindictive as the other, Beta just wanted a peaceful life. And he had to pay a price for that. Not him personally. That Asian had to be sacrificed. Beta paid the price of having to compromise on his principles. But that was ok. Who had principles in this world any way?

Beta knew his opportunity. It was now or never. He knew that the Son of the Emperor will come back to the area once he finished training. It would make no sense for him to go anywhere else when the father had painstakingly built up a huge empire of vascular surgery. And the father had decreed long ago that the area cannot have more than three vascular surgeons. Either he undermined and pushed Lambda out, or he would find himself the odd man out. And he was already not in talking terms with the boss, the big Alpha. It was very clear to him. The writing was on the wall. Either he acted now and protected his interests or he would be overtaken by events.

He knew how painful it would be when Alpha wanted to install his son and had to undermine Beta or Lambda. So he hatched a plan. He was waiting for his opportunity to complain about Lambda. That would give the boss the opening that he needed. A loaded gun. Lambda, being Lambda, was already carrying a chink on his shoulder in this community. Yes there was no overt racism in the country. That had been banned. But that meant nothing. If one had to target an opponent and he was of the wrong color, it was easy to motivate the staff to complain about that person. Nobody calls anyone the N word, or a paki, anymore. That was illegal. But there were ways to use the system to make life difficult for that person.

The system was loaded in favor of the ruling elite. The Shamans were a powerful lot. The politicians were afraid of them. The Surgical Guild selected the trainees in a centralized scheme, and also conducted the exams. The Guild or its proxies nominated the people who would represent the specialty on the regulatory bodies. The Guild also controlled the "external reviews" and "performance assessments" of doctors whose performance had been questioned. And the Guild or its proxy organizations also negotiated with the government to decide on reimbursement for procedures.

The health care in the country was a strange mix of public and private funding. Those who had the maximal lobbying power would obtain a bigger share of the loot. Radiologists, cardiologists and vascular surgeons competed for the same prize, or a share of it. The smart radiologists were able to have a very favorable system towards their specialty until the vascular surgeons realized that they themselves could do those procedures which were less time consuming than an average surgical procedure. This realization made a big difference to the income of the vascular surgeons. In this way the average vascular surgeon depended on the Guild to look after their financial interests. At the same time the same organization also was heavily involved in the selection, training and regulation of the vascular surgeons. Conflict of interest? What is that?

To cap it all, each state was divvied up into different health districts. Those who had appointments in the public hospitals had the cake and ate it too. They had opportunity to make a lot of money in the private sector. At the same time a public hospital appointment gave them legitimacy in the eyes of the primary doctors. For, when they referred patients to the specialists they did not have to check if the patient had private insurance or not. The specialist would have the option of treating the patient in either sector, depending on their insurance status.

Public hospital appointments were at a premium, for obvious reasons. And they were tenured for a period of five years. Every five years, the entire specialist work force had to have their contracts renewed. In most instances the renewal was automatic. But if the head of the department wanted to undermine someone, here was the opportunity. The politicians were too scared to disturb the hornet's nest. So they did not interfere.

Did we just describe a cartel? No. Absolutely not. It was all done for patient safety and for maintaining standards, or that was the reason given to Mr. Joe Public. Even the so called free press was reluctant to take on the system, unless individual doctors could be vilified. Horror stories sold papers.

In all these various functions or aspects of the Guild, it was a small group of persons who controlled the shots. They were playing musical chairs. One year one person would hold one position while the other another. But they would swap their places. Invariably the core group ended up being made up of the same personnel. This tended to be especially true for smaller specialties.

Add to this equation the fathers and sons. Some specialties had a disproportionate incidence of father-son combinations. Well perhaps the fathers inspired their sons so much that they followed suit, just like in the olden days when a carpenter's son became a carpenter and a builder's son became a builder.

Or was it due to selection bias? Was it an old boy's club? No one would admit that.

This was the dilemma Beta faced. There was room for only three on the boat. So the choice was between Beta and Lambda. That the father and son would be at the rudder was a foregone conclusion. Either Beta proactively pushed Lambda off or he would have to jump into the sea himself, when the time came.

He had delivered it on a platter to Alpha. First he initiated the complaint against Lambda. Then he had been at the interview panel to appoint the third surgeon, with Alpha staying out because of "conflict of interest." The son was duly appointed. It was all very legal. But the bloody Lambda had stayed on, practis

ing in the private sector. His continued presence in the region was an irritant and an embarrassment for Alpha. Now they have accomplished the second part of their plan. Chased him out. Got rid of him. The stupid fool did not know what he was biting into. He complained to the minister about the injustice. Now he would not be able to practice any medicine at all. And they were celebrating.

"Are you sure he can't come back? He was popular in parts of the region you know," remarked Beta.

"You don't know the nature of these things," said Alpha.

He paused for a moment. He was known to speak little. He was famous for preferring to communicate by emails than by talking. It was always hard to fathom what was going on in his mind. Perhaps his paucity of verbal communication was a tactic. Perhaps it gave him time to think up a measured answer. But it had a telling effect both on his friends as well as his enemies. It immediately gave him an air of superiority. It threw his adversaries off their balance. It also made a lot of people think he was very wise and knowledgeable, a virtual encyclopedia. But in fact there were many gaps in his knowledge and skills that those who were well nuanced could pick up easily. But then the majority of the people in the hospital and the wider society did not have the opportunity or the need to analyze him.

Beta was waiting. After a few seconds Alpha uttered the words slowly. "Once he is on the wheel like a hamster he will never be able to get off it."

He was not prepared to elaborate and Beta was not prepared to risk incurring his wrath by asking. Respect hierarchy and you will be alright, he thought to himself.

Alpha was correct. The medico legal process was complex. Once someone is smeared with the mud called complaint, it was nearly impossible for them to clear their name and get back to normal. Patient safety was a sacred cow. Once the specter of safety was raised, the Medical Board had to act. The first reaction was always to have a hurriedly convened meeting. Temporary restrictions would be brought with immediate effect, preventing that doctor from practising in a particular aspect of his field.

Then they would investigate. The investigations took several years. During this time the doctor would not be doing some types of operations. After a protracted investigation, even if the doctor managed to prove that he did nothing wrong (which is very unlikely, as fine combing the records would always bring out some thing, at least a punctuation error), several years would have gone by. All the while the doctor would be losing his or her skills. And by the time the case was finally heard, the Board would say that since the doctor had not performed those said procedures for a long time, they were compelled to formalize the restrictions.

It was a pathetic no win situation. And the legal costs would escalate with every passing day. Health care dollars well spent indeed. Ultimately the costs would be passed to the patients or the tax payers. Has this increased patient safety? This is debatable. And nobody cared. Because the ruling elite were untouchable, except when they were foolish enough to be involved in a case of criminal nature, such as sexual harassment, alcohol or drugs. The surgical standards and safety issues were only for the plebeians.

Then there were the oligarchs of other specialties and allied professions. They had their own Boards. There was always an indirect turf war between competing interests. But the unwritten rule was that the leaders of each pack would respect the right of the others to rule their own kind. Just like Kipling's Law of the Jungle.

Beta knew what it would be like if he was subjected to the ire of the boss. When he fell out with him several years ago, complaints came thick and fast. He was hauled before the Medical Board and restrictions brought to bear. He had nearly given up his practice. He ran away to another country. Finally he was back on board after a long time. But the scars had left him short of confidence. Certainly short of confidence and courage to stand up to Alpha.

Alpha always had his way. After demolishing Beta, he had gone around town saying Beta did very little, with his limited repertoire. The one area that Alpha could not invade was dialysis access surgery. For all his power projection, this was one area Alpha had neglected. There may have been a reason for that. Dialysis access surgery did not pay well. Most patients, who were on dialysis for chronic renal failure, could not afford private care. This immediately limited any potential financial benefit. Also the surgery involved suturing small veins to arteries. It required patience. May be it was not challenging enough. May be it was not glamorous enough to the show pony that Alpha was. Also the failure rate and requirement for emergency corrective surgery was high. It required a dedicated surgeon to do this. This was one area Alpha had neglected to get trained in, or practice. So he could not hound Beta out of this. But the brilliant chess man he was, he had a solution for this too. He got Beta to do all the access surgery. Being overwhelmed with this type of surgery, Beta was cornered in his own territory.

So much so that he started calling Alpha a psychopath. Of course it was behind his back. He wouldn't dare to say that to his face, even if they would have sat in the same room, before the new honey moon period started.

But now Alpha needed his help to bring his son into the region. That accomplished, he was not sure if Alpha would start his battle once again. And he was not going to give him a chance. He wanted five peaceful years. Then he would retire. Until then he would be on his best behavior. He would suck it up to the boss, and now his son too. He would swallow his pride, if there was any left.

"Do you think we crossed the line?" asked Beta, hesitantly. He knew that once a deed was done, Alpha did not want to dwell on it, especially if the deed made him feel uncomfortable. He was worried about the personal attacks that they had heaped on Lambda. He was also worried that they had said in their complaint that the vascular surgeons of the region did not want Lambda to practice in the region. Vascular surgeons in the region would include Alpha's son too. But he had not been a signatory to the complaint. Alpha did not want any focus on nepotism as the surnames were the same.

"Once we designate the complaint as 'mandatory notification,' we get a lot of protection from the law. We cannot be sued easily for defamation. Our allegations don't even have to be true," he paused strategically. Beta had to wait to hear him utter his wise words. And he waited with bated breath, as Alpha had left his sentence hanging in the air on an unfinished note, and his facial expression had indicated there was more to come.

"I will tell you a secret. If you question somebody's judgment, it is hard for them to disprove your charges. Judgment cannot be defined by the law. Then it becomes your word against theirs. And he is a Mr. Nobody here," he whispered. Beta had to strain his ears to hear the words of this wise owl. He had done it before and knew what works with the regulators. After all how could he have built an empire of this magnitude without having the cunningness and without knowing how to play the system?

Chapter 3

It was Friday afternoon. The dialysis nurse was looking at the time. It would be a few more hours before she finished her shift. She was looking forward to the week end. She had a dinner date with her boyfriend in an expensive restaurant in Big Smoke. Then they were going away for the week end. She had some inkling that he was going to propose. Otherwise why make this expensive dinner booking? They were both health workers trying to make ends meet and to pay the mortgage. They had little spare cash for indulgence.

The Big Smoke was an hour and a half away at best of times. With Friday night traffic it would be at least another half hour. That meant she had to get out as soon as her shift ended at 5pm so she could freshen herself and get to the date by 8 o'clock. Her boyfriend was working in the City and was coming directly from his work place. She had tried to get out of this shift but could not, as there was a shortage of staff.

She had told all other nurses on the shift that she could not stay late. They too had their chores. But they were accommodating. Theirs was the last shift for the day. Someone had to make sure that all equipment was safely switched off, then clean up and lock the center. Of course, the cleaners would come in the night but the clinical waste had to be disposed of properly. Today someone else had agreed to be the last person out. But still she had to make sure her patients were ok before she left.

The patients were connected to dialysis machines. A tube drew blood out of the patient for purification. The machines acted as the kidneys. The purified blood was then returned to the patients through another tube. The process takes several hours and had to be repeated three times a week. The patients who were able to, read or did computer work using the free hand, the other being connected to the dialysis machine. Some brought their music with them. Some brought their pets. Some just stared at the ceiling. Some were connected to EKG machines. The periodic sound of the machines had a rhythm to them. Once one got used to this, it was possible to ignore all the background sounds and be in one's own world. Not so for the nurses. They had to watch the machines for any sign of trouble. And they had to trouble shoot from time to time, a bleeding here, and a leak there; some patients needed more attention than others.

Due to the frequency of their visits and the length of each session, most patients came to know the nurses quite well. And they became friends with other patients. Yes there was a lot of camaraderie. The patients were united by the one common thread they shared. Irrespective of their back grounds, ethnic origins and religious beliefs, they were united by the fact that dialysis was their life line. They all had failed or failing kidneys. Some were on waiting lists for kidney transplants. Others had been deemed unsuitable for transplant. The latter had to have dialysis for the rest of their lives. Some would graduate to home dialysis, if they could be trained in that. Others would have to come to the dialysis center for several years.

Suddenly one of the machines started beeping. This was jarring compared to the background 'music' that they had all settled into. Which patient? Everybody craned to find out. And it happened to be her patient, of all the people! God! This had always been the case! Every time she was getting somewhere in her private life, something like this would happen! How many broken relationships? How many explanations? How many times has she had to cancel appointments? Now the potential proposal, potentially going up in smoke! Hopefully her partner would understand. He himself was a nurse.

Why am I getting ahead of myself? There is still time to sort this out before the end of the shift. She went to her patient. The tubes were shaking violently as there was some obstruction to the flow of blood. The machine was beeping in an increasingly loud manner. She was hoping that it would be a minor issue. Just a kink in the tubing or some similar mechanical problem.

As she checked, it was apparent that the patient's dialysis access had clotted. Dialysis access is the place where needles are inserted. It is usually a thickened segment of the vein, which had been prepared by being joined to the artery. In some cases a bridging synthetic tube graft implant is used to join to the artery on one side and the vein on the other. Needles are placed in this tube. This was not a preferred method, as synthetic tubes invariably get infected. Studies had shown that those using synthetic tube implants for dialysis had a shorter life expectancy compared to those who did not. Plastic tubes were also more likely to clot suddenly.

Murphy's Law never failed her. It had to be her patient on this important day and he had to clot off his synthetic graft! Now she had to solve multiple problems. Firstly the dialysis had to be stopped. Then she had to arrange for a vascular surgeon to review and take over the care of the clotted graft. Finally the patient would not have had dialysis since the Wednesday. She had to make sure his blood

Potassium levels were not dangerously high. It is the Potassium that kills. All this had to happen on a Friday afternoon.

She got on the phone. The switch board put her through to Dr Beta's office. Since the departure of Lambda, Beta had been doing all of the dialysis access surgery. "He is overseas on holiday. It will be another two weeks before he returns. You need to call the on call vascular surgeon." Beta had left strict instructions with his secretary.

So back to the switch board. The on call surgeon was the son. Well it was actually Alpha who finally answered the call. The son was away in Big Smoke. He had two jobs. The job in the city was his primary interest. But the father had wanted to get him appointed in his own area so that he could hand over the tens of thousands of patients in his books to the son. He was not going to give away this impressive number of patients to someone else. With the patients came the periodic ultrasound exams for life. 'Once a vascular patient, always a vascular patient' was Alpha's motto. In fact it was 'once my vascular patient, always my (or my son's) vascular patient.'

That left them with a problem. While the son loved the hustle and bustle and the glamor of city life, the father was left straddled with his patient loot, unable to let go. This caused frequent over lap of on call and other commitments. Invariably the father ended up holding the on call phone for the son. It was all good for the short term. But what the father did not seem to appreciate was that he was getting on in age. In his mid sixties he was being on call two thirds of the time. Workaholic he may be. But how long could he cheat nature?

And he had limitations. He did not do dialysis access surgery. This was one area he had not been interested in. When he recruited Lambda a few years back, he made sure that the new person was interested in doing dialysis access surgery. At that point in time he was planning to undermine Beta to make room for his son.

"Dr Alpha here" was the terse reply at the other end of the line when the telephonist had finally managed to locate him, operating in a private hospital. He was silent till the nurse explained the situation. Several times during the call she was not sure whether he had hung up on her or not. Finally he answered.

"I don't do that type of surgery and we don't offer that type of emergency service. You call his nephrologist." His voice was cold and emotionless. He put the phone down. He was not interested in this patient and it was not his problem.

"If Lambda had been still here he would have come in straightaway. Whatever his faults may have been he was fucking prompt," said one of the other nurses.

The nurse in charge was less enthusiastic about Lambda. "Before Lambda came to the region Beta was the only surgeon doing this surgery. When Beta was on holiday we simply did not offer this service. So we are back to the same situation. What is the big deal?"

The big deal was that the nurse had a duty of care. She could not walk away from this patient without handing him over to some one. And her dinner date was slipping away with every passing moment.

The nephrologist too was not very helpful. "He needs to go to Big Smoke for this. And we can't send him there on a Friday night. They would be overwhelmed with their own problems for the week end. We cannot send him there."

He ordered her to arrange for the patient to be sent to the emergency department. Hopefully one of the doctors there could insert a central venous catheter into his neck veins. Then he could have dialysis over the week end. There goes my engagement, she muttered. No one was taking ownership. Neck lines were also quite prone to get infected. They also caused problems such as narrowing of the veins due to reaction to the synthetic catheter which could lead to long term problems. The lower the number of central venous catheters used the better the quality of care in the dialysis center. In fact it was a key performance indicator. But that did not seem to matter. Nor was her private life. Nor was the fact that if the patient's clotted graft was not declotted soon, he could permanently lose that access. That meant he had to start all over again with a new access in another area.

But it also meant that Beta would be busy when he got back.

Chapter 4

The sonographer was tired. Her right wrist was aching from pressing on the probe on the patient all day long. Her back was hurting from being seated on a stool the height of which could not be adjusted, all day long. This day was a particularly tough day. There were many exams for varicose veins. This would involve the sonographer being bent on her back for extended periods. The cubicle was small. This was her world for the day. There was hardly any room for her to move. The space was barely enough to accommodate the patient's couch, the duplex ultrasound machine and a small desk. If she leaned back she would be touching the back of the man working on the other side, separated only by a thick curtain.

And the boss had insisted on doing fourteen examinations per day. All of the sonographers had to comply. There were three others in this site. The boss operated some satellite centers in other parts of the region. If Dr Alpha detected the slightest dissent or discontent he would send her to one of the far away places. That would mess up her daily routine even more, with long drives at both ends of the day.

Absolute loyalty and dedication was demanded. If anyone was slightly out of line, they would be made to regret it. She found that out the hard way. Once before, she had hung a favorite painting on the wall in her small work space. After all, this was all she would be seeing all day, except for the short lunch break when she was allowed to go out. The boss did not like anything on the walls. He wanted the environment to be bland. There should be no distractions. Otherwise the work ethic would suffer. That was his motto.

The next day when she came to work, the painting was gone! Yes it was missing without a trace. None of the other employees were forthcoming with any information when she enquired. There was a chilling silence. Finally she approached the boss.

The normally stoic Dr Alpha exploded. He was annoyed that she had hanged the picture without his permission in the first place. And now she had had the gumption to ask him where it was. "It's in the bin!"

"But, Dr Alpha this is a painting my husband and I have cherished for a long time."

He looked straight into her eyes. Was it hatred or a show of power? Whatever it was, she did not like the look at all. As per his habit he was silent for a few seconds. Then he started, "If you cherish that painting you should keep it at home where you can look at it and relax. This is work place. People come here to work, not to relax."

He continued "This is my castle. Nothing moves here without my authority. If you don't like to work for me you are welcome to leave. But remember, it will be difficult to get a job anywhere in the country if you leave on bad terms. But if you want to work for me you should do exactly what I ask you to do."

Having said that, he returned to staring at the computer, not even acknowledging her presence any more. That was the ultimate insult. She did not exist anymore in that moment.

Cold bastard, she thought. But she did not dare to say it. She left the room quietly to return to the dreariness of the mechanical work, without any time for reflection on what she was doing.

Dr Alpha was not always like that. He could be charming. Especially when someone talks about sports, he would regale them with several anecdotes. He had been a sportsman in the past. In the presence of outsiders, especially government officials, he could be a very bubbly person, talking about his favorite sport. But the coldness always showed through if one cared to look deeply.

She hated her job. But she knew she had no alternative. Another sonographer had fallen out with him when Alpha wouldn't let him take his pregnant wife who had broken her waters, to the hospital without dropping off the office laptop on the way, as it had some of the previous day's work. Alpha took pride in being a strict disciplinarian. But the sonographer couldn't take it anymore. He resigned. Only then did he realize that in the small vascular world, wherever he interviewed, they would pick up the phone to Alpha. And he would kill the job. After being jobless for six months, with a newborn baby to boot, the person had to go overseas to find a job. When he eventually returned to the country after a few years, he had to work in far away places and rebuild his professional network of acquaintances before he could come back to the region, this time with a radiology group.

And she knew about the fate of another colleague of hers. She too could not work with Alpha anymore. She resigned and was looking for a job in the Big Smoke. That was about a year after Lambda came to town. He was trying to establish his own vascular laboratory. And his offices were close to where she lived. When their interests coincided, they opened a vascular laboratory. They soon started providing high quality service to the patients of the region. And to cap it all they did not charge any deductibles or co payment. The government rebate was enough for them to break even and make a small profit. Lambda was naive when he thought he could play the old fox at his own game. He was oblivious to the ground realities. That was when things started to go sour for Lambda. Finally he was booted out of the region, thanks to complaints. The lady who had the courage to defy Alpha was left without a job.

That is just desserts for those who did not play the game according to the rules, eh, according to my rules, thought Alpha. And everybody in the region knew not to cross his path. Every single person who challenged him met with an unsavory fate.

Alpha was a very talented person no doubt. He knew that anticipation and adaptation were the critical needs in a rapidly changing field. Gone were the days when vascular surgeons just did surgery and left everything else to the radiologists. Vascular surgery, in fact, was part of general surgery. It came under general surgical departments most of which were headed by gastro intestinal surgeons. These chairmen had no idea of the needs of the vascular surgeons when that specialty itself was moving rapidly towards the minimally invasive endovascular surgery, which involved treating the arterial blockages with balloon and stents rather than bypass surgery. Technology and equipment were evolving at an alarming rate, expanding the role of endovascular surgery enormously. The old time vascular surgeons were left behind while those who got on the bandwagon and were able to learn the new techniques quickly, were able to consolidate their positions and market share. The specialty itself became separated from general surgery.

Once vascular surgery was established as a separate specialty the pioneering surgeons realized that they wielded enormous and unmitigated power. Being a separate but small specialty meant that those who were technically adaptible and were politically savvy were able to form their own society. It was all about protecting their exclusivity. Of course they were doing it all for quality assurance. The office bearers were all a small group of people who would exchange their job designations every few years.

And the politicians had to consult this small group, be it approving new equipment for purchase, deciding on government rebates for procedures or appointing personnel to committees including regulatory authorities. And the surgeons too became politically savvy. They realized what they had been missing out on all these years, with the radiologists cardiologists and other specialties already using lobbying power to advantage their own specialties.

As soon as they got recognition as a separate specialty they formulated credentialing processes for the ones to follow them. The objective of course was to maintain standards. But it also gave a few unscrupulous individuals the chance to unfairly build empires.

Hard on the heels of the endovascular revolution, or perhaps starting even prior to that was the revolution in piezoelectric technology. This enabled powerful ultrasound machines to be built, the imaging capabilities of which were now nearly as good as CT scan and MRI. Ultrasound is minimally invasive and has no known hazards to patients such as radiation. Soon ultrasound became an extension of clinical examination, thus becoming an integral part of vascular surgery. So much so that modern day vascular surgery cannot be practiced without a reliable ultrasound service.

Again the enterprising vascular surgeons realized that they could learn the nuances of interpreting vascular ultrasound themselves. Soon many of them started to open their own vascular labs. In this they had to share the spoils with the radiologists. The radiology practices usually had multiple modalities of tests under the same roof. And they practiced in large groups, unlike vascular surgeons. But the laboratories opened by vascular surgeons had a boutique like feel about them. And since the vascular surgeons themselves reported on the scans, they would be able to make clinical decisions straightaway, unlike the information being relayed back and forth between specialists of different kinds. This was similar to echocardiogram and EKG services run by cardiologists.

Having his own vascular lab helped Alpha in two ways. Firstly it was a money spinner. Though the government rebates were quite generous he charged a co payment. Secondly being the only vascular surgeon in town with his own vascular lab raised his profile among referring doctors. Also as the quality was good, they were obliged to refer the scans to Alpha. And when there was an abnormality detected on the scan, Alpha would write back to the primary doctor and at the same time take care of the problem too. This meant the primaries had a one stop shop. They could refer and forget about the patient. Many of them liked it. It also served as a means of attracting new patients.

Alpha, who had near zero interpersonal skills had found a way to ensure a steady flow of referrals through ultrasound. And many of the vascular conditions such as aortic aneurysms, needed periodic surveillance scan. This meant that once he had built up a critical mass of patients the ultrasound work would be self generating. He had found a wonderful business model.

It was a totally different scenario that developed for Beta. Both Alpha and Beta were exposed to the same changing environment in the specialty. While Alpha adapted and expanded, Beta retracted. He was not into learning the new skills at that age. So he developed the attitude of an ostrich, the bird he had become fond of lately.

At the beginning Alpha and Beta had practised as partners. But as he trained himself in endovascular surgery and also got new qualifications in ultrasound, Alpha realized that he was propping up someone whose practice was dying. They had started an ultrasound laboratory together. But Alpha was well aware that it was his skills and hard work that the practice was running on. In fact Beta did not have any qualification on paper that would enable him to sign off on test reports. This was his chance to take control. Alpha ensured that someone complained to the Medical Board about Beta trying to report on ultrasounds and also doing endovascular surgery. Restrictions were brought on Beta. Life became so tough for him that he left his practice to go overseas for more than 6 months. When he returned Alpha had usurped the power and was the emperor of vascular surgery for the region.

Building up such a practice of enormous volume also had its drawbacks. It was like holding a tiger by its tail. Alpha could not take holidays or go away for any extended periods, for fear of losing his grip on the referrals. Also he did not want to be accused of abrogating his patients.

So there he was working almost every day till late into the night, and not having any vacations. Beta called him a psychopath, of course only behind his back. He could not face any more retribution from this powerful man.

Chapter 5

The face looked familiar. He was trying to work out where he had seen her. She was wearing shades and had a burqa on. It was not a garment covering the whole body. Rather it covered the head and the upper body only. The face was open but the sun glasses were quite dark and he couldn't see the eyes properly. The rest of the body was exposed. She was wearing denim jeans. The upper half of her was conservative and the lower half very modern. She was wearing high heels to complete the totally anachronous attire. She was walking very confidently. Was she a conservative Muslim? Her demeanor appeared out of place. And her shape and something about her looked very very recognizable. She walked past him in a jiffy. And she was gone.

"Who is she?" asked Lambda, from the receptionist. "We are not allowed to discuss clients," was the terse reply. He should have known. He was a doctor. Patient confidentiality is of utmost importance. Well he was not really at a doctor's surgery. He was at the office of a psychologist. Not something that he would have imagined in his wildest dreams. But here he was, seeking counseling. He did not want to attend a local therapist. He had come all the way to Big Smoke, hoping that no one should see him. He had sought out the most expensive psychologist, who exclusively treated up market clients only.

Then it struck him. The burqa. Surely that was a disguise to conceal her true identity. Who was she? He was sure he had seen her a numerous times. But he just wasn't sure where it was. Perhaps she was a minister? Or a politician? Senator? What would they do if they needed psychological support in their high pressure jobs? Obviously the psychologist was not going to do house calls for all of them. Some had to come to his office. And if they were living in Big Smoke, they had no option but to cover their identity and hope that no one would see them. In fact the psychologist office was strategically placed in a corner of a shopping mall. People could roam the mall for a while and quietly slip into this office without raising alarm.

The burqa was a good idea. Why didn't he think of a turban or some scarf to cover his head? There should be no stigma attached to visiting a shrink. Nearly one in five people had mental illness according to statistics. But it was easier said than done. Still people did not want all and sundry to know about their problems. In the era of Instagram and Facebook one never knew when they would end up as a viral video.

He went in when it was his turn. The office was unconventional compared to his own. There were very comfortable leather settees, glass top tables and flower vases. There were many paintings staring at him from the walls. They were mostly abstract art and he did not understand most of it. There was one piece of Picasso, obviously a copy, which he recognized. But recognition is one thing. Understanding is a totally different matter. Like everyone else he too looked at the paintings pretending to appreciate them. The ambience was more like a hotel lounge than like a doctor's office. There was some soft classical music playing in the background.

"What can I do for you?" asked the therapist. Lambda poured out his heart to this man. He was a professional. Working at the high end of the market he was accustomed to seeing doctors, especially surgeons who are overcome by stress at various stages of their lives. Some had marital problems. Some had affairs. And most had workplace discordance.

"In the current day work place, there is a lot of pressure on the doctors. Especially if you are a proceduralist you have pressure from all around you," said the therapist. This was his opening gambit. He waited for Lambda to continue the conversation.

"Pressure I can absorb. But not when I have a psychopath as boss."

"Everybody thinks that their boss is a psychopath," intervened the therapist. "You are not the only one!"

"It is not only my opinion. Dr Beta has also said the same." Lambda was confident that his diagnosis was correct. That was actually the consensus before Beta swapped sides and did him in. Or rather Beta caved in and made him the odd man out.

"Besides," continued Lambda. It is not just dealing with a psychopath. It is also dealing with a nepotizer in the same person."

This certainly caught the therapist's attention. Nepotism in the public sector in this day and age? This was unusual. What was this man talking about? In his thirty six years of practice he had seen it all. Nepotism in the private sector, yes it was rampant. But in the public system in this day and age of transparency? His interest was piqued. But he was clear in his objectives. He was not going to be involved in the rights and wrongs of the situation. He was only going to help his client cope better. But as a human being he couldn't but help thinking that some thing terrible, some thing gravely unfair, had happened to this doctor.

Justice is one of the factors that determine happiness. The psychologist explored various aspects of Lambda's situation. Yes there were financial worries; yes there was loss of face and tarnishing of reputation; yes he was having sleep problems. But the most important issue was Justice. That someone could do this to another person and get away scot free. That was the main reason for Lambda's unhappiness.

Without getting emotionally involved the psychologists probed Lambda's mind further. What would be the ideal resolution of his problem? What would make him feel normal? At the moment Lambda felt as though they had cut off a part of his body. He felt incomplete and inadequate.

"There is no justice in the system," said Lambda.

"Apart from coping with the situation, which is your first priority, is there any place or any agency you can complain to?" asked the therapist.

"Sure there are. But justice is only for the connected." Lambda knew he was up against a Mafia. He had no chance.

"But you should try. There are many agencies that can investigate into corruption." It would give him some hope and some target so that he could focus his mind on that. The therapist knew that Lambda had zero chances against a cartel of conniving people who had a vested interest in protecting each other. Together they would stand. That seemed to be the motto in these types of situations. Truth seemed to be the last thing anyone was interested in, except perhaps the victim. For the others it was all about keeping the appearances of a fair and just society. As long as they don't see themselves in the newspapers or on television they could continue the status quo. They were not going to sacrifice one of "the boys" to grant justice to this outsider.

But he had to try. Hope is what makes life tolerable. People move from one hope to another. When their desired outcome doesn't materialize humans quickly revise their targets. Then they have fresh hope. That keeps them going till the next disappointment. This is the cycle of life.

The Buddha had said desire is the root cause of all unhappiness. He should have added that hope is the root cause of all happiness. The have-nots have hope as their only possession. And they are happy. The haves have everything they desire. But they desire more and are unhappy.

In any case having faith in the system is crucial for this man's mental health. Otherwise he could rapidly deconstruct and self destruct his life.

"You need a reset button. Focus on what you have to do, rather than what you have lost." With these words of wisdom he sent away his charge, asking him to come again the same time the following week. People needed many sessions before they could move on from the acute grief state they were in.

Lambda was busy trying to settle the financial matters. He did not want to declare bankruptcy. He put his house on the market and gave notice to the landlord of the office. He had to terminate his employees and negotiate with the companies that sold him hi-tech machines to get them to buy back with minimal losses. It was a nightmare situation that he wouldn't wish even on his worst enemy. 'Why did they do this to me?' was the thought that crossed his mind frequently.

He was caught in a bind. He was trapped by the lease terms and loyalty to employees, and of course. his patients. Had he known that Alpha had a son whom he wanted to install in his place he would never have taken up this job. Alpha's son was in training. And had it not been for the fact that he had set up the practice at such cost, he may have run away at the first sign of trouble. He had been fooled. He did not read the writing on the wall correctly. Perhaps he was viewing them through colored glasses. Yes. Alpha had been a hero to him. He had so much love and respect for this man who was considered one of the leaders of the field in the country. In fact Alpha had been elected President of the Vascular Federation. He too had voted for him, although he wondered at that time why these affairs which are usually decided unanimously, had to end up in a vote. Perhaps Alpha had enemies within the Federation and was not popular among the profession. Alpha had just scraped through. Now he regretted voting for Alpha. When the majority was less than fifty, every vote would have been worth two.

And he had Hobson's choice. When he first had problems he met Alpha, trusting him totally and utterly. Alpha had probed him about the clinical cases that were reviewed, promising absolute confidentiality. "You can tell me anything. Tell me what actually happened. Nothing you tell me will leave these four walls," Alpha had said, with a disarmingly sincere look. He encouraged Lambda to tell him anything and everything about the cases. In retrospect Lambda now understood that he had fished for dirt on him. But there was nothing he had not told others that he could tell Alpha. He shuddered to think, what may have happened if there was in fact some explosive confession. Alpha would have had no qualms in using that against him at the correct opportunity.

And he was not sure when to actually challenge the injustice he was being subjected to. It was all in the name of patient safety. And Alpha had offered to help him through this crisis. He knew he was like a lamb being led to the slaughterhouse. But until Alpha's sudden turn around and until he openly turned hostile, and until he installed his son in Lambda's position, there was no open confrontation. And Lambda, though he had severe misgivings, had to play along. Because, he thought that Alpha's son would be an idiot to be saddled with two jobs as soon as he finished his training. It was customary for the trainees to go overseas, spend time in another center, and return with a well rounded personality and wider repertoire of surgical skills.

So Lambda had not protested or complained about his treatment. He did not want to antagonize Alpha and Beta who would continue to be his colleagues after they reinstated him. Because of Alpha's deceptive behavior, and his of own naivety, he did not raise the alarm bells till late. By the time he realized that he had been hoodwinked, he had missed all the legal deadlines to bring an unfair dismissal claim against the hospital.

Once he knew that he had lost the public hospital appointment to the son of Alpha, he wrote complaint letters to all and sundry. But Alpha was too savvy for all this. All Lambda had to show for his efforts was a so called "external" review by the hospital which white washed the appointment process. How stupid had he been? He had continued to work in the private hospital, hoping that justice would prevail. Not in this so called land of fairness. Alpha's hand was everywhere. His tentacles reached the private hospital as well as the politicians, regulators and everybody who could help. How stupid had Lambda been? His overheads were killing him. In order to make ends meet he had done short locums. He should have known that he would never get justice. He should have cut his losses and left long ago.

In a way Alpha had not given him a chance to leave honorably. He was backed up against the wall. His only way was to fight back. But it was Goliath country, and he had no chance.

Chapter 6

While keeping busy with the practical aspects of winding up his practice one thought always occupied the back of Lambda's mind. He had to find out who this woman was. Was she really Muslim or was she only trying to hide her face. He had definitely seen her some where. He knew it was unethical to try and find out private details about patients. But then he was not her doctor and he had no boundaries imposed by his work ethic. Secondly he was not even sure if she was a patient. She may have been just a visitor to the psychologist's place. Somehow he felt a compulsion to find out. It helped to distract his mind from the reality of having had his licence taken away from him. It was definitely therapeutic to indulge in some thought other than the overwhelming feeling of anger, craving for vengeance and a sense of grave injustice.

Perhaps fate was in his favor. Perhaps everything had been cast long ago and he was just acting out the script. Or perhaps he was making his own destiny. The next appointment also coincided with the visit of the object of his curiosity. Hoping to get a glimpse of her he arrived very early for his appointment. It was not that he knew hers would be just before his. But he was hoping. If she was a famous socialite trying to get away for therapy on the sly, why would she choose the same time every week? That would make her a sitting duck for nosy paparazzi that could lie in wait to ambush her. But on the other hand she could be a working woman whose schedules could be the same for most weeks. In which case this could be the only time she could get away safely. Yes it was a blind shot. But in the mentality he was in, even the question of would she be there or not helped to wade away some of the negative thoughts. It was just a game. And a harmless game.

As he waited out side in the waiting room, lo and behold! There she was, coming out of the psychologist's chamber. Same dress, same head dress. For a second their eyes met. Her eyes were blue; hers was not the gaze of a woman who belonged to a culture which forced women to cover up. Rather her look was that of a very confident Western woman. And he got a fleeting glimpse of her hair this time. Yes she was blond! He knew for sure that this was a woman wearing disguise to hide her identity.

He was shaken from his trance when the receptionist spoke to him. "The doctor has to attend to some urgent business. He can see you in an hour. If that's inconvenient we can reschedule the appointment."

This was a golden opportunity! He was not going to waste it. "I will be back in an hour!" He was almost out the door as he finished the sentence. He ran after the woman.

"Miss you dropped your pen," he panted as he called after her. She was a fast walker. She had covered more than a hundred meters by the time he caught up with her. In his energized expectant situation he could have beaten Roger Bannister. That's how fast he ran.

She stopped momentarily to say "It's not mine. I did not have a pen on me!"

"But the pen dropped off your dress. I saw it falling." He was insistent. It was like he knew better than she did, of what she was carrying.

"That's strange. It's definitely not mine. You can have it or you can return it to the office." She turned back and resumed her walk. She was not in a mood to start a conversation. And he did not know how to proceed.

But he had heard her voice and her accent! Now he was sure he had seen her somewhere. In fact he had seen her a lot of times. Though he could not place her immediately, he had made a lot of progress in his investigation. It was only a matter of time before he would uncover her identity. Mission accomplished. At least partially. He congratulated himself as he walked slowly back to the office. Small victory. That was all he could expect with the way things were in his life. If she did come again the following week he would definitely strike up a conversation. He had to first guess her identity. He had seven days to figure out. Having been stopped in his tracks suddenly from a busy working life these small challenges seemed to be the only joys in his present life.

The psychologist must have noticed he was not concentrating on the session. But that was understandable. Anyone who had undergone such harrowing experiences would exhibit difficulty in concentrating. That was normal.

"Do you have any suicidal ideas?" asked the psychologist all of a sudden. Lambda was not expecting this. Taken aback, he said "What if I said yes to this question?"

"Well if you tell me you have serious suicidal ideas, I will have to terminate this consultation and inform the authorities." He was very matter of fact. "We don't want to lose any life, leave alone that of a trained doctor."

Lambda knew this was a game. The psychologist was covering himself. If he said yes he would be packed off to a mental health facility and put under suicide watch. And the Medical Board would then make it even more difficult to get his licence back. It was a catch twenty two situation for him. He was sure many doctors would have faced the same situation. And would have hesitated to reveal their innermost thoughts.

"Of course I am not suicidal" said Lambda, with the conviction of a python that was caught swallowing a long stick. The question was out of the way. The therapist was safe now, and Lambda had avoided another hurdle in his professional life. Everybody was happy. Sigh of relief all round!

He thought he had just dodged a bullet. In fact he had thought of suicide briefly when things began to unravel for him at an alarming rate. But he had willed himself to carry on because if he died, he would die as an accused. He would die a tainted surgeon. Yes now he was a painted surgeon who was a surgeon only on paper. But at least he had a chance to clear his name. He was not going to give up until he obtained justice.

He returned to his pad, and was having dinner watching television. He was flipping through television channels absent mindedly while munching through his dinner. He had lost his taste buds with the advent of the bullying episode. He was eating for the sake of eating. Eating to live. In fact he had lost some weight lately.

Suddenly something piqued his interest. A flashlight went off in his brain! Yes! The girl! Rather, the woman! It was the same woman he had seen in the psychologist's office. Same eyes and same voice. Now it all made sense! Yes she was a television presenter. And she was certainly not Muslim. She had attended the clinic in disguise to avoid the stigma of being labeled with a diagnosis by the press.

What more can be interesting in his life? He was a painted surgeon. He was not allowed to practice. In a life of such boredom and drudgery, discovering the identity of the mystery woman was equivalent to watching a James Bond movie in the sixties. This was the most exciting event to have occurred in his life in many days. Such a pass his life had come to. The once busy surgeon was now like a beached whale. But the key difference was that the whales had more rights and more well-wishers than an accused surgeon, no matter what his contribution had been in the past.

The next few days just lapsed. Was he in a prolonged perpetual state of meditation? Time just stood still. The past, the present and the future seemed to be fused into one continuum of blackness. Nothing seemed to be happening in his life. But the woman's face seemed to haunt him. He definitely wanted to talk to her. He wanted to ask why she was there and why she was so secretive about that. He looked forward to the next appointment. Would she be there? Would she have finished her counseling sessions? He was determined to do something that would allow him to know more about her.

The next week arrived soon enough. In the intervening days he started watching her programs regularly. "I am becoming obsessed with her! This is not good for me," he told himself.

Well there he was, half an hour early for his appointment. Waiting anxiously. Was he infatuated with her? Or was it just curiosity. But he was hell bent on mounting his latest hobbyhorse even if it turned out to be a buckaroo!

"Excuse me miss, may I have your autograph?" he said as he caught up with her, walking briskly from the office towards the car park. She was in her usual garb. She slowed down slightly but did not stop. Avoiding eye to eye contact, she mumbled "You must be mistaking me for someone." She continued to walk, and in fact started to increase her pace.

"That thing you said about Donald Trump is totally wrong. He is right in asking for a Muslim ban!" he said, as tried to gather his wits and somehow prolong this conversation.

He had done well. This caught her attention. When someone believes in something passionately, they would react instinctively when that subject is broached. And the television lady was no different.

"How can you say that? How can you brand an entire religion?" She had stopped, and was looking into his eyes.

"I know you are not Muslim. So why do you get so emotional about this?" He asked.

He had her ears. "Can we talk about this somewhere else?" she asked. She was resigned to the fact that her camouflage was no longer working. And this man did look like an intelligent well informed person. And he had the wrong ideas in his head. She wanted to convince him.

"Let me cancel my appointment and join you in the car park." She told him which level she was parked in. He ran back into the office to change his time to another day.

Chapter 7

"Ok I am the woman from television. You are correct," she said as she sipped her cappuccino. He had ordered black coffee. They were in a cafe, in a corner, shielded away from the prying eyes of the passers by. "And you?"

"I am a painted surgeon!"

She laughed heartily. "You are funny! What does a painted surgeon do? Are you an artist? I have heard of tree surgeons and the like. Everybody likes to call themselves surgeons. They don't realize how much time, effort and sacrifice goes into the training of a surgeon."

"A painted surgeon does nothing! And I am a painted surgeon for sure."

"Are you a religious missionary of something? How can you survive doing nothing?" She looked puzzled.

"I am a surgeon. A surgeon who underwent the hard work and training that goes into the making of every surgeon. But I have been barred from practising my trade. My license has been suspended. So I am now a painted surgeon. I am just like a picture of a surgeon you will see in museums. Just like the painted ship on a painted sea in Ancient Mariner. I do nothing!"

"I am sorry to hear about that. And you don't have to tell me. But I hope you didn't rape a patient or molest a child? I can handle if you were caught drunk at work or was under influence of drugs. But I can't handle sexual predators." She knew that this man appeared to be a decent bloke. Surely he must have done something horrendous and criminal. But there are some types of crime that she could forgive and some that were unforgivable.

"Oh no no no! Nothing of that sort. I had a complication and the patient went to a hospital where I did not have privileges."

"Can they take away your licence for that? That is unbelievable." She looked at him with suspicion. May be he was hiding something from her. Well if he was going to hide anything why should he reveal that his licence was taken away, in the first place? Something was wrong.

"Oh yes. They can take away the licence for farting in the operating room, if they want to. It is draconian. Shoot first, and ask questions later is the attitude."

"But how can they do this without a proper reason. This is a momentous decision that will change your career forever."

"Well that is the law. In the name of protecting the patients they can do anything!"

"Who are they? Is there a panel of several people who decide this?" This was supposed to be a democratic country. Surely there have to be many people who would deliberate thoroughly before taking such a punishing decision.

"You will be surprised! When I passed my surgical exam there was a court of examiners comprising of a dozen surgeons, many of them well respected professors, who grilled me in all aspects of surgery before allowing me the privilege of being a surgeon. But when they took away my license there were only two people, one of them a lawyer and the other a middle grade surgeon, not a top notch professor, who decided this."

"Oh I am sorry. I thought bullying occurs only in showbiz!"

"You will be surprised. If I tell you what happened to me you will write a novel or make a television program."

"But when two people take this momentous decision, isn't there any scrutiny on their actions? Don't the other doctors review these decisions?"

"Not as far as I know. There is no automatic quality control. I can appeal. That's all."

"How can you go about appealing?"

"Well I can appeal to the same people. Biased as they are, I am not confident I will get justice. Then there are courts. But courts can only lift the ban or leave it in place. The courts cannot impose conditions or restrictions when a doctor is banned, as opposed to modifying conditions imposed by the Medical Board. That means most judges are reluctant to do anything about the ban."

"Besides," he continued. "There is another agency that looks at the complaint in detail. They take months if not years to either charge or exonerate the doctor. It is like parallel mirrors. One agency bounces you off to the other and then back. Then it gets lost in the court system. So, though the initial ban is supposed to be only temporary until all the matters are investigated, it effectively finishes off the career of a doctor. He is financially broke. He loses his patients. He loses his referring doctors. Even if he wins the case, they will say he cannot practice now as he had not performed the operations for many years. So in reality there is no justice."

"We should expose this. This is worse than the Soviet Union or North Korea." She was the television personality always on the look out for stories of injustice.

"People have fancy titles and wield big weapons. But they lack the substance and the maturity that one needs when using weapons of career destruction. And there are no timely checks and balances."

"This is like a communist dictatorship!" she said.

"Furthermore there is a small cartel that controls the specialty. If we fall foul with the members of that cartel we are finished. It is the same group of people who select trainees, examine them, give medico legal reviews and sit on Medical Board committees. "

"What about the press? Surely we have a free press. That should highlight any injustices?" As a media person she had a lot of faith in the power of her own organization.

"The press is only free for the plebeians. Not for the ruling elite unless they start fighting among themselves." He was very pessimistic of all the institutions of the society.

She pondered for a moment. Then said slowly "Yes the media too is controlled by vested interests. It is hard to get your story out if you are fighting the establishment." She paused a little and then said "You haven't asked me why I was seeing the psychologist."

"If fact I was only curious to find out who you are and to confirm my suspicion. Beyond that I have no interest in gossip. I don't need to know why you are undergoing counseling."

"You did not hide anything from me. So I better tell you too." She must have felt that sharing her problems with someone could ease the burden.

"If you insist." he said. "I am a good listener and I am totally non judgmental."

"That's good to hear. What you are going to hear will shock you." She started on her tale of woes. She was a television news reader and program director. And she worked in an organization which was hierarchical and misogynistic. The attitude seemed to be similar to the attitude in operating rooms thought Lambda. It was nothing new, though those in power would never admit it.

A beautiful woman working amidst a group of hungry men would invariably be targeted by some one. And the person whose attention she had attracted was one of the senior vice presidents.

"I could have easily said yes. And I may even have got a promotion. Life would have been good. I was not even in any relationship. It would have been easy to go with the flow. I may have had a sugar daddy and I may have had protection against other suitors once they came to know I was so and so's property." She sighed.

But she was not someone who would compromise for expedience. "How could I have done what he was asking, and continued to respect myself. How could I have looked at myself in the mirror eye to eye?"

She refused. And she complained. If she had just refused and kept mum she may have survived the episode and perhaps not suffered any consequences. But she complained. That's when her life in the organization started going awry. She complained because the company policy clearly stated that sexual harassment was taboo. It was banned. There was zero tolerance for that. And the poor woman had believed in that. She had the nerve not only to refuse this powerful man, but also to complain about him!

They went through a process. The Human Resources did everything by the book. Yes they had an inquiry. And the defendant challenged her to prove her allegation. In a world of power politics who would stand up for her? Who would risk their own careers to be her witness, though his behavior was quite blatant and public. She could not prove her case. At the same time the predator brought his own counter complaint against her. She was accused of fabricating her story to discredit him. She was sent on compulsory leave for a few weeks. Lambda now remembered that there was a temporary stand in for a few weeks until the regular newsreader returned from 'vacation' as claimed by the television channel.

She was asked to undergo psychiatric evaluation. Her duties were reduced, though she was still allowed to read news, which she absolutely loved. And she was required to undergo ten sessions of counseling.

"You are lucky," she smiled. "This was the last session and I would not have been there next week. " Thinking to herself for a few seconds, she added "I should say I was lucky. I would not have had a chance to share my woes with an understanding and non judgmental person if you hadn't tried to confirm my identity. I am really glad we met."

"In my case there was threat of losing my personal boundaries if I had acceded to his demands of sexual favor. But in your case couldn't you have sucked up to your boss and survived?" She wanted to know if he could have handled his situation better.

"I have often thought about it. But when a person is determined to bring his son into my position and when there is constructive dismissal evoking 'patient safety' I had no chance. At least now I can hold my head high and fight back. The boss is a psychopath and is not in touch with reality. Even after acting in such a disgraceful manner he probably believes his own lie that he did everything for patient safety. His son just happened to be in the right place at the right time!"

He then explained very briefly what had happened to him, and how there was a witch hunt to find some dirt on him that would stick.

"It is too painful to recollect what happened. I will explain that at some other time," he said. Every time he thought about the injustice that was perpetrated on him, his heart rate would go up and he would be overcome by an overwhelming sense of grief and negative thoughts.

"You must fight back. I will do everything within my power to help you. Take care of your health." With these words they parted. This was the beginning of a friendship or relationship that would see them getting deeper and deeper in to each other's problems over the coming months. They told each other that it was only a platonic friendship. That they were only helping each other because they were in similar situations. But was it true? Why were they getting more and more emotionally involved. Could two people sharing negative experiences create a positive energy between them? Two negatives should create a positive according to mathematics. But does this apply to human emotions?

Chapter 8

"So are you ready to talk?" asked Gamma, the girl.

"If you are ready to listen I am ready to talk." Lambda was now over the sharp emotional numbness that he felt soon after his licence was taken away. He could now talk about the events from the point of view of a spectator. It was like it had happened to someone else. He was merely a witness. Whether it was the counseling or whether it was the friendship of Gamma, or whether it was just the healing effect of the passage of time, he felt different when talking about the most traumatic events of his life.

What started as an idle curiosity had now become a full blown friendship. There was nothing physical, at least not yet. A friendly peck on the cheek or an occasional hug were all that transpired in that sense. But emotionally he felt a becalming effect. And he needed that. She too seemed to love his company.

At first they had studiously avoided the topic, that of the reasons that culminated in both ending at the therapist's office. They both knew that the other had been treated unfairly. But they were not ready to go into details. They just liked hanging out with each other.

She was the first to open up. She described how the predator tried to groom her, sending her on out station assignments and to far away conferences where he would invariably show up. These travels came with perks. Business class air tickets, luxury hotels and the rest, at company expense. Exotic destinations, fine wine and gourmet cuisine could be intoxicating to any aspiring career woman. And she did enjoy all that. But the perks came with strings. The suitor was always present. And would slowly inch his way towards her physically.

The giddy heights of power and money would tempt anyone to make compromises and adjustments so that the status quo could continue. Any wrong move would upset the apple cart and the cost to her career would have been quite significant. As long as there was no physical intimacy Gamma did not mind an old fool making silly jokes and making himself look like an idiot. The others in the organization turned a blind eye. They had seen it before. There was a culture of acquiescence. Behind all this was a climate of fear. Everybody was scared of losing their job.

Gamma played coy and hard to get. The sexual predators actually enjoy the chase as much as the prize. It was only after they conquer their targets do they lose interest in them. So the more Gamma resisted or dodged the more attention she got. It would be a lie to say she did not enjoy the advances to a certain extent. She was not a prude by any means. But she had her boundaries.

All was well until the day of reckoning finally arrived. Sending her for a premiere in Las Vegas, the chaser mysteriously turned up. That was ok, she could handle that. But when he made his move on her she realized that now was a fork point in her life. Either she compromised and played the game according to high society rules, or she stood her ground and openly decline him. She chose the latter.

Then the repercussions rained on her like a tonne of bricks. Her position in the organization became almost untenable. Having created a series of problems for her the villain moved on to a more amenable target. Gamma's life had become a living hell. Daily meetings, strict reporting requirements and removal of many privileges. The negative cascade of events followed swiftly one after the other. Human Resources were of no use. They were a well oiled machine the purpose of which was to minimize risk of litigation for the organization. They were simply not interested in justice. If she believed in the harassment policies of the institution that were shown to her when she started, she now believed that these were just empty words designed to satisfy a legal requirement. Any one who complained would be marooned in a sea of red tape that was supposed to ensure fair and transparent process for everyone concerned. But in reality these were shrouded in complex legal jargon and were of no use to real victims.

Her choice was to accept the solution offered by the management, which was really a demotion with a requirement for counseling. It was the only option left for her short of leaving. Any legal battle would be time consuming and costly. She was not ready for that. It was not a challenge to be taken on by one person alone. Though there were many in her situation each was isolated and prevented from liaising with others by their own different circumstances.

Each disillusioned employee was suffering individually and biding their time for better opportunity in other organizations. They needed references and other vestiges of good will from their current employer. So the bullies continued to be bullies and the victims continued to suffer in silence. That was the hard reality that she had to swallow. Meeting Lambda was a welcome development. She now had something other than her career to think about. And someone who was in similar situation to compare notes with. Misery loves company they say. But their motivation was not to wallow in their mutual miseries but rather to help each other cope better, and fight the injustices done to them.

Initially they had shared only neutral information but as the confidence in each other grew, and as the memories of traumatic events became less painful, they were able to share more details of their dilemmas.

"Where do I start?" asked Lambda. It had been a long drawn out case of bullying and mobbing.

"Once upon a time.." smiled Gamma.

"Ok I will start. Nothing but the truth and the whole truth," said Lambda. "Nothing else will do," said Gamma. She was afraid if she was developing feelings for this man, who looked very sincere and was devoid of any pretense. She knew she was not ready to handle his problems on top of her own. But she somehow wanted to help him. He would feel better if there was someone who would listen to him. Who knows she may even be able to help him see his own problems in different light. After all as a television personality her job was indeed to help people see all sides of the issues.

They had gone on a week end getaway. Two rooms. No hanky-panky. That was the condition. They were sitting in the balcony overlooking the beautiful harbor, with the setting sun providing a golden back drop. They were sipping red wine and nibbling on the chicken wings and nuts. Such idyllic setting! But they were discussing the life changing events of grave magnitude!

Perhaps the relaxed atmosphere encouraged both to be free and frank. He said "I have worked in many countries. But the politics, corruption and nepotism in this country are unbelievable. I can't believe that they allow this to happen in a democratic country like this!"

"Okay. I was on call. A patient with a stab wound to the left side of the chest was brought to the Emergency Room with extremely low blood pressure. The left lung field on the chest x-ray was a complete white out. I rushed the patient to the operating room and as soon as he was anesthetized, made an incision across the chest. We managed to control the bleeding. This patient went home in 10 days, without any neurological deficit. This is a patient who would have died with any delay in treatment. But I was criticized. They made complaints against me.

"The head of the department said I should have done a vertical incision through the mid line, bisecting the breast bone. This is called a sternotomy. This is the standard way to expose the heart. But it takes time to split the bone. What I did is called clam shell thoracotomy. The chest is opened across just like the name implies. Here, only in the middle part of the incision do you have to cut through the breast bone. In any case it was an emergency situation and you just have to get in there as soon as possible and fix the bleeding.

"They even said I had difficulty in closing the breast bone. I am not a strong man and you have to drive stainless steel wires through the bone. I may have had difficulty but I am not ashamed of that. This is not an operation that you do every day. The fact of the matter was that we got in quick and stopped the bleeding, and the patient survived. But that seems to be the least important issue.

"Then they said I needed to have done a time out."

"What is a time out?" Gamma had been a silent nodder until then. He was glad she was asking for clarification. That showed she was listening attentively.

"A time out is a procedure where everyone in the operating room introduces himself or herself, then the patient is formally identified and the site and side of the operation confirmed. Then the surgeon explains what the operation is about, and airs any anticipated problems. The others too mention their roles and potential issues that may crop up."

"Isn't it a good idea?" asked Gamma.

"It is a great idea. It has been shown to improve complication rates and performance. And I did explain to the team what we were going to do. But I am not sure if there would have been enough time to do a formal time out. The head of the department said "You should have stood back and taken a deep breath. And do the right thing. It doesn't matter what the outcome is. If the patient dies. so be it." But I don't think that is correct.

"I think the patient would have died. And then they would have blamed you for that too," smiled Gamma. "My dear Lambda, the die had been cast. What ever you did or didn't do, would have been wrong. When someone wants to eliminate or sideline you, they can always find something."

"Listen to this too. They said I raised my voice and that I was incoherent. That was the icing on the cake. They said I have to go for communication courses."

"Wow! You communicate perfectly well. Could they not understand your accent?" asked Gamma.

"I am normally very soft spoken. But in an emergency situation I may have raised my voice. It's like you are in a war zone. The adrenaline is pumping. You are in a fight or flight situation. There is no time for niceties." Lambda sounded dejected.

"Did you go for communication classes?" asked Gamma.

"Yes I did and the instructors were surprised that I needed training."

"Were they racist?" She had to ask. She was a television reporter. She looked at issues from all angles.

"Possibly. I don't know. Racism in the hospital system is not like racism in the wider community. Nobody calls you names. It is more subtle than that. People are wiser. All I can say is that the only people in the operating room who were of different color were the patient, my assistant and I. The ones who ganged up against me were all of the same color. But I cannot prove that race was the prime motivation."

"The underlying bias would have contributed, no doubt," said Gamma.

"I was at a mortality audit some time later. And they presented a case that died at another hospital. It was similar. Stab wound to the chest. The doctor on call had no experience in opening the chest. So he went vertically, to the left side of the breast bone, where the ribs attach to the sternum (breast bone), cutting each rib individually. The patient died by the time they got in. "

"Was he criticized?" asked Gamma.

"Far from it. The audience comprised of experienced surgeons and professors. They said "Well you are not a heart surgeon. You tried your best."

"Wow! Accolades for one and brickbats for the other? You are a shit magnet. You seem to attract all the nasty people!" Gamma looked at him affectionately and squeezed his hand. "A delightful shit magnet!"

"If you thought that was it, you are wrong. They made me do a performance assessment."

"What is that?" asked Gamma.

"They watch you consult with patients and watch you operate. But that was the easy part."

"What was the hard part then?" asked Gamma.

"The hard part was urinating in front of a woman!"

"What?" Gamma nearly choked on her wine.

"Out of kindness of heart they want to check if you have any health issues before they put you through the performance assessment. And they check you thoroughly mentally and physically. And they do lab tests too, check your vision, hearing and what not. They also check you for drugs!"

"No wonder! You were incoherent and did not close the bone quickly!" laughed Gamma.

"Fuck you! Don't laugh. I was treated like a drug cheat. I had to urinate in front of a witness so that I did not change the urine sample. Like I was an Olympic athlete. And they were so considerate they sent a woman to witness my urination!"

"That's outrageous! Was she pretty?" asked Gamma.

"Stop joking. I was not in a mood to look at her face. They talk about sexual abuse all the time. I can imagine what would have happened if I had an erection!" Smiled Lambda, resignedly.

"You would have missed the sample bottle and overshot!" said Gamma. Hey I couldn't help joking. But seriously, this is atrocious. You should have complained!"

"Yeah right! I complained. And they just delayed my performance assessment, sure enough they tendered an apology. But words are cheap. So in effect my protests only served to prolong my agony."

"You should sue them!" said Gamma.

"Sure, they would have turned it around and said I made a move on that woman!" Lambda couldn't help being cynical. He felt that the whole system was loaded against him.

"You must have felt humiliated. Any other person would have quit by then. I have to admire your resilience!" said Gamma.

"I cannot quit just because someone doesn't like my face or someone wants to bring his son in my position. I owe it to my parents who educated me and my teachers who taught me. I cannot let all those years of hard work to be taken away at the whim of a small group of people."

That was all he could talk about that day. The rest had to wait. Reliving those traumatic moments was extremely painful and anxiety provoking. It was very unpleasant. He did not want to talk about his harassment anymore on that day.

The wine and the soothing music combined with the kind and pretty face of Gamma served to assuage his feelings. He was back to his normal self soon. He was a fighter. He was not going to let these bastards win.

The dinner was very nice. He was conscious about reducing the carbs. So it was mostly protein and vegetables. But she insisted on a desert. "I love the chocolate cookie crunch trifle in this hotel. I cannot let this opportunity pass," she said. "You should try some too. You can have your work out later'" she winked.

He was not sure what she meant. Was she hinting at something?

They had said to each other that theirs was only an intellectual friendship. Nothing else. But as they came to know more about themselves they began to like each other a lot more. Gamma was beginning to worry about Lambda. She had worried about friends in the past. But this was different. It was not just about the present. She was worried about what would happen to him. About the future. Did they have a common future? She had never thought of settling down. Now she couldn't put aside the thought that may be, perhaps, this was the man she had been waiting for all these years. Just a fleeting thought. But a thought nevertheless, and a repetitive one at that.

"Did you want to come for a night cap?" asked Lambda.

"I sure do'" she said. She did not want his company to end quickly. She suddenly felt lonely. She could not sleep. She did not want to sleep.

He went to her room. They ordered some gin to the room.

"I am getting drunk," he said.

"This is only your second glass," she said. "I thought surgeons could last longer."

Did she mean some thing else? Or was he imagining.

"I am drunk on thine eyes," he said, peering into her big beautiful eyes. Indeed they were worth drinking to, and the two were drinking on.

"It's the booze talking" she said. She was mighty pleased that he had noticed yet she chose to play coy.

It was a fact that at that point in time she was the person who knew most about his innermost secrets, mental agony and career problems. And he was the one with most knowledge of her torturous past. They were closer than ever before. Both knew this would lead to something further. If only one of them took the lead and initiated proceedings. Both waited for the other. But neither made a move.

"Do you think I am a bad surgeon?" he asked after a long silence.

"Not on the evidence you have given so far. But I have to listen to the whole story."

"Ha ha you will be bored to death," he said.

"No! Everything you do and say is interesting to me," said Gamma. They hugged each other spontaneously. Is this the moment they had both been waiting for? She melted in his arms. The night became very long indeed.

There was no work for housekeeping in his room the following day. Saving the environment? If they had helped prevent global warming by even a trillionth of a degree they had released a lot more heat into the atmosphere by their physical exertion. Life is like this. A gain in one front and a loss in another.

Chapter 9

The morning after was difficult. Lambda was overcome by guilt. Had he exploited someone in a vulnerable position? He was not able to offer her a life with him. Not until his name was cleared at least. And he did not want to give her false hopes of a long term relationship.

She stirred in her sleep and turned towards him. "Are you awake?" she asked. She continued "Don't worry I won't follow you till the end of the world. Absolutely no strings attached, I promise."

In a way he was disappointed that she did not think of him as a long term prospect. On the other hand he was relieved. She was sportive and would move on.

"Listen," she said. "I just like you. I like your company. And I am intrigued by your situation. I want to help set it right for you. But does it mean I love you? No! Not at this time any way. So let's take one day at a time without thinking too much about last night!"

"Did you enjoy it?" he asked, hesitatingly. "Of course! You are good at what you do and you know how to cherish a woman."

"But let us be just friends for now. Let's work through the issues in our respective careers and then we will see how we feel about each other." With those conclusive remarks Lambda bundled away all thoughts of sex to a side and started to focus on the tasks at hand.

"Don't you have any organization that you can complain to? Surely there must be a code of conduct?"

"Oh yeah! There are codes and there are codes," smiled Lambda. They even have competencies for surgeons. In theory each of these competencies is important. Not just medical knowledge and cutting skills. Among these competencies are communication, cooperation, team work and professionalism. Unfortunately these are observed in breach more often than not!" Lambda was pessimistic.

"But unless you make a complaint they won't know. And unless they know they can't act!" Gamma was insistent.

"I did call. I spoke to the vice president of the Guild of Surgeons. After listening to my tale of woe he just said "These are employment matters. We won't get involved in them."

"Vice president again! Screw the vice presidents! The source of my trouble was also a veepee!" screamed Gamma.

"If you had screwed the vice president you wouldn't be in the soup you are in now!" smiled Lambda.

"Fuck you! There is a time and a place for jokes. Some topics are out of bounds!" said Gamma.

"Sorry if I hurt you. Didn't mean it," said Lambda, meekly.

"Okay let's come back to the subject. I think you should go there, plonk yourself at their doorstep, and ask for justice."

"They are in another city. I don't want to go there!" He was making excuses.

"No, you are going." There was an air of finality in her tone.

"I will go if you go with me." He was holding out. Perhaps he wanted to try his luck.

"No chance! I am well known. I couldn't even go to see my therapist wearing a burqa without being noticed." She looked at him piercingly. "Do you think we can fly together and meet someone at a high profile place without setting the tongues wagging? You are a big boy. You can look after yourself!"

That being decided he was ready to tell her more about his problems. "There was a case where another doctor was looking after a patient with arthritis. The patient was plied with steroids. As you know, the steroids make normal people susceptible to get life threatening infections, as they suppress the immune system. In course of time this patient had infection of the heart valves, called bacterial endocarditis. The patient was sent to Big Smoke and had a heart valve replacement.

"After the heart operation the patient had pain in the abdomen and a CT scan revealed a small infected aneurysm in one of the arteries to the gut. The doctors there elected not to do anything immediately. The patient was sent to our town with arrangements to have vascular follow up here.

"The infectious diseases specialist, who was supervising the antibiotic treatment rang me one day, requesting me to see this patient urgently, as the patient had presented to the Emergency Room multiple times with belly pain. A CT scan showed that this patient's aneurysm had more than doubled in size. In a patient who is on blood thinners following the heart valve replacement, the danger is that if this aneurysm ruptured, he would bleed out and die.

"So I prepared him for surgery. Looking at his scan I could see that his aneurysm was in one of the smaller arteries and not the main gut artery. So I was confident I could handle this. Even so I arranged for a very experienced general surgeon to be present in the operating room in case the patient needed resection of part of his bowel. In retrospect I could have just shipped him back to Big Smoke.

"In any case there we were, trying to get time in the operating room on a Friday, which is near impossible as it is always busy. Then the Head of the Department of Anesthesia rang me and said " Can you do this in one of the smaller hospitals?" You see, our area is big and there is one bigger hospital, which we may call Small Smoke, and another slightly smaller hospital, which we can call No Smoke. The facilities are almost equal. I was worried that if I do not agree, the operation would be postponed and the patient's aneurysm could rupture over the week end. So I agreed. My operation went off very well indeed.

"Later the patient developed problems with his original heart operation and they had to redo that operation in Big Smoke. The patient had a prolonged and complicated recovery from the heart operations. But they blamed me for doing this operation locally and not sending him to Big Smoke. Also they deliberately falsified facts and said that I operated on the main artery to the gut, completely ignoring the CT scan evidence staring at their faces that this was not the case. No one questioned the doctors at Big Smoke why they sent this patient back without treating the aneurysm. Nor they were scrutinized for not doing a good job at the first heart operation.

"In fact the infectious disease specialist who referred the patient to me, remarked several months later "Lambda, yours was the only operation that went off without any hitch. Every other operation or treatment that this patient had was fraught with complications and problems." Yet I am the only one who is being penalized!"

"That is absurd. So who makes these decisions and why don't they give you a chance to correct the mistakes they made?"

"Absolutely not. They sent what was called a draft report. And that was sent to the Medical Board in the draft form. There was no natural justice!"

"Hmm. Are we in North Korea? Even there, there will be some process unless you have become a personal enemy of Kim."

"Well when Kim wants to bring his son in my position and I need to be moved away, what else do you expect?"

"How did you cope with this," she asked.

"Well if I gave up, that would be a complete betrayal of the trust and effort placed on me by my parents and teachers. It will also be letting down my patients."

"So did the patient complain?" she asked.

"Not really. The patient, or more accurately, patient safety, is a weapon in their devious schemes. They care about the patient as much as they care about me!"

"Why is the press being silent?" she asked.

"You know how you were treated in the media industry. Unless there is some incentive for the top brass, these things get pushed under the carpet. The press is an instrument of mass control. They can only function within a certain ambit. These things go to the very core of our society. They are hard to fix. Corruption and bullying are inbuilt in the system. Any attempt to change that will upset the apple cart. And the politicians don't want that. I mean politicians on both sides."

"But we cannot let this go unchallenged. You should fight till the last neuron remains in you. They can harm you physically. They can hurt your career by various rules and regulations. But they cannot shut you up. They cannot control your thoughts." They both had a common cause. A common purpose. Lambda had gone up in her esteem. The fight was on. They were up against the entrenched powers in a rigid system. But if no one fights injustice, this world would be a horrible place. There would be no Davids if the Goliaths are accepted as unbeatable.

He made plans to go and meet the Guild of Surgeons. She had a busy schedule. They would not be able to meet for a couple of weeks. He missed her. For the first time in a long while he was missing a woman. It was not the physical craving. It was the intellectual companionship that he missed. And here was a person, for a change, who was willing to listen to his point of view. The general attitude was that there would be no smoke without fire. So the doctor was guilty until proven otherwise.

He had to prepare his brief when he visited the Guild of Surgeons. He wanted to take as much evidence as possible with him so he could convince the powers that be that a great travesty of justice was being enacted. And enacted in their name, by their members. Will they listen? Or will they side step? Will they offer a solution or will they dismiss his case outright? They were the ones who made the policies, which for an outsider, still looked very fair, transparent and professional. Yes they were the ones the public looked upon, to uphold the standards. Will the standards be the same for everyone or will there be double standards? There was anxiety, trepidation and hope when he embarked on the journey.

As if to reflect on his mental state there was a very heavy downpour in his town. He was worried that his house would be flooded. In fact many areas around his town had been flooded already by the torrential rain. The rain continued for days. He felt like Noah. Noah without a boat. He had to take a train to the airport. He was not sure whether the train services would be operating. He was trying to watch the weather channel on TV but even the television blacked out for a long time. Such was his luck lately that he believed his trip was going to be cancelled. Well he was used to disappointments. He was ready for more. A storm causing travel disruption would be the least of the problems confronting him.

He went to bed having set the alarm for an early start. He found it hard to sleep with all the worries and anger swiveling in his brain constantly. When he finally fell asleep it was past midnight. He was worried that if he was not rested his performance would suffer. But there was nothing he could do about it.

He woke up to the chime of his alarm clock. What a difference a few hours sleep could make! He felt refreshed. He was confident. He felt energetic. And the weather too had cleared overnight. The sun was coming up. The skies were clear. Not a cloud to be seen anywhere. If he was worried that there would be falling branches and trees that would stop the trains, this proved not to be the case. He had hope. Hope that a person who would listen and understand his situation, and would be moved enough to act.

Chapter 10

The whole atmosphere was daunting. The Guild was housed in a prime real estate area. The campus was huge. In modern economic sense they could have rented out their premises for millions of dollars. Or they could have sold the land and downsized. They did neither. They just kept growing. Every year there would be new departments and new employees. It was an empire that kept expanding. They had their tentacles in every aspect of a surgeon's life.

The Guild charged huge subscriptions which would eventually be set off against expenses by the individual surgeons. So indirectly this behemoth was being subsidized by the tax base of the entire country. In this era of internet and Zoom communications, everything could be done from a small premises in a remote area. What was the need to sustain this ancient institution at such expense, Lambda wondered. It was a symbol of authority. And it was supposed to be the symbol of quality. At what cost, wondered Lambda.

The lucky few who had become office bearers tended to play musical chairs, swapping and hopping from one position to another culminating in Presidency for few. There had been an outcry, and nowadays the elected officials tended to change frequently, and recycled less often. Then there were some who managed to transition from being a practising surgeon to become a salaried employee of the Guild. And there were plenty of opportunities for those who had managed to entrench themselves in the top echelons. This was a nice retirement plan for some.

All this was supposed to contribute to patient safety. Whether it made any difference was anybody's guess. But it did give some individuals enormous power over the lives of surgeons. This was an empire. There may not have been one Caesar, but nevertheless there was no denying that this was a kingdom. All man made empires would crumble one day, thought Lambda. When would this become dust in the wrath of righteousness, thought Lambda.

Every time there was any public scrutiny, the Guild would move heaven and earth to maintain the status quo. It was adept at manipulating the press. It had friends in high places. The anti competition regulators could not touch it. When there was out cry about bullying, the reaction of the Guild was typical. They devised a course about bullying that all the surgeons were required to complete online. That ticked the box. Once a surgeon completed this, he would not bully. So said the Guild. Then it had a bullying hotline that was supposed to be accessible to anyone who felt bullied. These created new positions and new directorships. More superannuation plans for the lucky few at the top. Did it really make a difference to the victims? Lambda was about to find out.

These were the corridors of power in Surgery. For whom and by whom was this created? Certainly it was not by the patients and for the patients. Yes the patients are the very reason for the existence of surgeons. If there were no patients there would be no surgeons. Beautiful buildings. Wonderful awe inspiring surroundings. For whom? And by whom?

The mantra in the Guild seemed to be respect for hierarchy and military discipline. Keep a stiff upper lip and grin and bear. Don't challenge authority. In a way Lambda felt he was entering a Freemason Temple.

But he had faith. Surely all their written policies were not an attempt to hoodwink the public? In the era of face book and twitter how could an organization which was like a dinosaur in his opinion, survive being exposed? The problem was not in the bullying itself. It was the system that created the atmosphere where bullies could thrive with impunity. If the same group of people could influence selection for post graduate training, conduct examinations for board certification, advise the government on policies, and appoint surgical representatives in regulatory bodies, it placed an enormous amount of power in a few individuals. To add to this the Guild often sought to interfere in appointment committees for surgical positions, as well as in reviews of complaints against a surgeon's practice.

Such power should come with a lot of responsibility and should be wielded with total transparency. When he counted the disproportionate number of sons and fathers in the specialty Lambda couldn't but help wondering how this was possible. Perhaps all the sons get inspired by their fathers. How could it be anything but this. How dare he think otherwise?

He had made an appointment with the Director of Bullying. The appointment time was 10.30 in the morning. He had arrived half an hour early. He was greeted by a pleasant personal assistant to the secretary to the Director of Bullying. In fact the department had many employees. Their prime task of course was to administer the on line bullying course. It was added to the boxes that needed to be ticked before one became a surgeon. Yet others were manning bullying hotlines. Could they not have done all these from home?

"I will make you a cup of coffee," said the PA, as she directed her subordinate to make coffee for this doctor who had chosen to visit them in person rather than just call. The new girl took his specifications and went to the coffee room. "Would you like to have something to eat?" she asked just before leaving on her errand. "Have you had breakfast?"

It was not for pleasantries or food that he had traveled all the way from another city. Why am I being cynical? They are just trying to make me comfortable, he thought. He hoped to wrap up everything and leave on the last flight of the day. He had booked this as a day trip. He had not booked a hotel. He had come straight from the airport. In a way he was grateful that these people were hospitable. But the real test of their sincerity would be when there was real action about his grievance.

At 10.35 the Director of Bullying appeared. Quite a rotund lady, she had a very pleasant demeanor to her. She apologized profusely for the five minute delay.

"We don't like to keep our clients waiting. We know how important and precious every minute of your time is." She was all smiles.

My foot, he thought. Was she being sarcastic? Having lost his licence, he was unemployed. He had all the time in the world on his hands. There was nothing productive that he needed to do. Zilch! Absolutely nothing, except to prepare his defense against this unprecedented assault on his career, his character and his entire persona. Defend against allegations that he thought were false and unfair. This was not how his time was meant to be spent. He was a trained surgeon who was meant to be helping patients. He was supposed to be tending to the sick. But instead he was left counting sheep in the clouds of smoke arising from his burning career.

"Thank you for being so considerate." He smiled at her his charming smile, the smile that his patients loved, prompting some to call him the 'smiling doctor.' Only this was an empty smile, not the genuine caring smile that he would give his patients.

He repeated his tale of woe. He had spoken over the phone before. She knew the basic facts. But she wanted him to repeat it all to her. She seemed disinterested or distracted as there was not much eye contact or head nodding that he would associate with active listening. But different people had different body language. He could not say for sure if she had actually taken in what he said.

When he tried to go into clinical cases she stopped him. "We are not doctors. So there is no point in repeating this to me."

There was an awkward pause. It was obvious that she did not want to be there. She had to somehow go through the motions without appearing to be disrespectful. That was her challenge. Respect was the catchphrase these days. Respect colleagues; respect staff; respect clients. At least appear to respect.

Lambda was not sure if she was actually interested in what he was saying. But he had no clear evidence that she did not pay attention. It was not like he could pause and ask her "What did I say last?" This was not the occasion for that. So it turned out to be a monologue. A monologue of his woes.

It had started quite innocently when the medical director had written to him "There were concerns about your performance." No details were given. But the director had said they were going to get an external review by the Guild of Surgeons. No details had been given. He was well liked by his patients and this took him by surprise. The director had said "The review is to see how we can improve the performance." It was not supposed to be punitive. Still he had no indication about what cases were going to be reviewed and why. Several months passed in a state of limbo. Whenever he asked for an update the standard answer had been that they were waiting for the Guild of Surgeons to draw up the terms of reference and to nominate the reviewers.

There were many versions of the terms of reference. No one seemed to know which one was the correct version. When the reviewers finally arrived, new cases had been added to the one or two cases that were drip fed to him over the several months of waiting. It was a mess. He had no time to prepare his defense. Then they went into recess. For several months he was kept in the dark. He now believed that they were playing for time to enable Alpha's son to complete his training, and were taking things close to the time when Lambda's contract was up for renewal. Lambda would have no time to fulfill any required corrective action recommended by the reviewers. Then he could be removed and the way could be paved for Alpha's son to make a grand entry.

It was so crafty that Lambda could do nothing but watch things unfold. On the one hand he could not antagonize the management overtly other than protest meekly through his lawyers about the delays. On the other hand he knew that he was being led to the slaughterhouse. He had set up practice and employed people. He could not walk away from it all suddenly even if he wanted to. It was like playing a game of chess without your queen. He knew that Alpha could check mate him at a time of his choice. Alpha had the power of life and death over his career.

He still believed in the goodness of people. Had it been an all out war he would have known exactly where he stood from day one. But this was a shadow war. Alpha was nice to him on the face of it. He told him that he was trying to help him. And Lambda had no choice but to accept this. He was hamstrung by his financial obligations. It was like he was in a prolonged nightmare, being frog marched into oblivion. And he had absolutely no power to stop the events.

One of the clauses in the terms of reference was that if the reviewers saw anything dangerous they would stop the review and notify the Medical Board. "They didn't stop the review. That is a good sign," said one of the administrators.

When the draft report finally arrived it contained many factual errors. He had asked for a chance to respond. But Lo and behold! The medical director had promptly forwarded the report, with all its errors, to the Medical Board. There was no natural justice. It was like he was riding in James Bond's famed Aston Martin. Suddenly the eject button had been pressed.

Still on the outside they were all very polite and smiling. In fact Alpha called him to his home. He had a nice informal chat including talks about ball games both loved. "I can't believe the report," he said, "I need to write to clarify some things with them. But the fact of the matter is that they have asked you to undertake further training in open aortic surgery. I would strongly advise you to abide by that."

"I am happy to do that. The whole life is a learning curve and I am happy to use any learning opportunity that comes my way," said Lambda. "Will you take me under your wings. May I scrub in for your cases?" he asked, pointing to the fact that there was going to be no formal trainee allotted to the hospital for the following year.

"There may not be any trainee but I still have a junior doctor doing the job. He has sacrificed his personal life to join my unit and I owe it to him to train him." said Alpha. It was a load of humbug, thought Lambda. Open aortic surgery was very rare in the present age. Is this guy going to train a totally raw fresh graduate straight after internship to do open aortic surgery? But when Alpha had made up his mind, no one could change him.

"Besides," mused Alpha. "If you scrub for my cases it will not look nice and the nurses won't respect you."

As though the nurses at that particular hospital respected me, thought Lambda. But when Alpha pronounces his decision, and justifies it with his own logic, however lopsided it may be, that was the end of discussion.

"You need to go away to another unit for three to six months. Then you will be able to turn it around." Alpha sounded a bit positive. For a person in Lambda's situation any inkling of positivity appeared to give hope.

"I am not averse to going away for three months. But I have a lot of overheads. Who will look after my patients? Who will pay my expenses?" asked Lambda, not wanting to appear to be adamant but at the same time not wanting to be walked all over completely.

"The Guild of Surgeons have said you need further training. So the onus is on them to find you a suitable position. But I will try to help you. For this to work both of us will need to be absolutely honest with each other. I will copy you in on all my correspondence and you should do the same."

Then he spoke about different units in the country and also in other countries. He seemed to have a wide network of friends. As long as one was under his wings, his friends would be helpful. The moment he was left out in the cold the very same network would strangle and snuff out any life left in his career. Lambda realized that he was well and truly in the clasp of this man. The man, who purported to be his friend and mentor, wielded a frightening amount of power over his life. Luckily this man is not a sex pervert, he thought. He shuddered to think what may have happened if he had demanded sexual favors. He would not have been in a position to refuse.

After talking about other things for a while to relax his prey, Alpha dropped the bombshell. "I have a solution for your practice too. If you comply with my instructions I may ask my son to do your locum for you. It means your patients will be looked after, and you will end up making a small profit!"

Profit? My foot! He was struggling to make ends meet. Alpha had a tight control over all the referrals in the region. Lambda remembered the instances where Alpha had willingly given him patients. They were invariably patients with gangrenous toes who continued to smoke and who did not have any suitable vein that could be used to bypass the blocked arteries. And of course they had no private insurance. This was very different to the places he had worked in previously, where the senior doctors would give nice cases to the new boys on the block so that they could notch up some successes that would boost their confidence, and also establish their credentials among the staff. But here it was different. Alpha would work till ten at night so that he could do all the operations himself. He had no life outside. And the cases that he passed on, were doomed to fail. They were also traps perhaps. It was to make him walk on a minefield so that he was set up to trip up.

With such iron grip on the referrals this man was talking about profit. But Lambda was not in a position to analyze and make an informed choice. His choice had been made for him. He just had to follow.

When he had the job interview he was asked "Is there any questions you would like to ask the panel?" He had said no. He had been advised that it would not look nice for him to ask questions from his potential employer. If he had asked for information, that might have indicated that he had not done his home work about the job. And if he had asked about other aspects such as salary, hours of work etc that might have shown him to be a greedy or difficult person. In future interviews I will have to ask from them "Does any of you have an offspring that you may want to bring into my position?" Well it was too late now. The son had been plonked right in the middle of the equation.

Now that the son had been brought in, the priorities changed. The priority went from giving Lambda the additional training that he was supposed to need, to fitting everything to suit his son's agenda.

"My son will finish training in three months. So I want you to wait till he is available before you go away." That would be beyond the date of expiry of his contract, which, for all practical purposes, was not going to be renewed automatically now. Once he lost his foot hold and Alpha's son gained a toehold on the job, Lambda knew his own position would be precarious. He would go from being the incumbent to being a non entity. Whereas Alpha junior would become the incumbent and the heir apparent, if and when there was a competition for the permanent job.

"He won't apply for the permanent job. He will leave when you return." Alpha must have sensed his trepidation and struck a reassuring note. "It is in your best interest to keep this all in-house. If we allow an outsider to come in, that person may want your job and you will be in a far worse situation."

Did he have an option to say no? It was like North Korea under Kim. "Yes Sir" was all that was expected of him.

Yet in spite of all the red flags he trusted Alpha would do what was right by him. He was a big star in the Guild of Surgeons. And they had benchmarked surgical competencies which included professionalism, team work and cooperation. How could a man who was supposed to espouse, and stand up for, values of continuous professional development and a lifetime of learning, back stab him after sending him for 'further training'? It was unimaginable that such a possibility existed.

In spite of his forebodings Lambda embraced the idea with enthusiasm. He would go to another center, make himself better for his patients and return triumphantly. And Junior Alpha, who was now well and truly in the picture, would move out gracefully. He could even arrange for Junior to follow Lambda for this additional training. When a surgeon travels he acquires a polish that local training could never impart. This was true for any country. Whether he learns newer techniques or not the very fact that he lives and works in another country would make him a more rounded surgeon. Perhaps Junior could return to Big Smoke as a professor. That is what any father would want for his son, thought Lambda. Who would want his son to do exactly the same as his father, in the same small town. Every generation had to go further than the previous generation, thought Lambda. So what was right by Lambda would also be right by the Junior. So thought Lambda. It would be a win win situation for all.

If he thought everything appeared to be getting better, little did he anticipate what was to come. The initial honeymoon period was quite cordial. For some reason Alpha preferred to communicate by emails rather than phone calls. In a way this left a trail of irrefutable evidence for the future. But at that point emails from Alpha were the highlights of his days. And he joined Alpha in 'grand rounds' where they saw all patients under both of them, once a week. The grand rounds was followed by teaching sessions for medical students. Lambda felt alive during these sessions. Yes he loved teaching.

If Lambda thought his troubles were going to end, he was mistaken. Initially everything started to move smoothly. The medical director told Lambda that on expiry of his five year contract he would be placed on short term locums until he completed his additional training. He waived his legal right to protest against the non extension of his contract. He did not have to, but challenging that would have placed him on a confrontational path with Alpha. There was no possibility of entering into a legal battle when Alpha held all the strings.

And Alpha copied him in on his correspondence with the medical director where he introduced "my son" into the mix. "We are trying to help Lambda," he had said. Am I being subjected to daylight robbery of my career? wondered Lambda. But he was voiceless and powerless, watching this drama being enacted in his name, at his expense.

For his part Alpha arranged for Lambda to go overseas to another unit. The doctor at the other end had told that he could come any time. But Alpha wanted him to hold out until his son finished his training and a planned holiday. So he had to wait for three months.

Then the trouble started. He was like Sinbad with the old man of the sea sitting on his shoulder. First, Alpha wanted him to grant Alpha direct access to the Medical Board in matters regarding Lambda. "This is highly unusual," warned Lambda's lawyer. You cannot give him a carte blanche." So citing his lawyer's objection Lambda politely declined to accede to this request. Then came the three month - six month debate.

"I don't need this training in the first place," protested Lambda. "I am happy to go for three months but not six months."

"My son won't come unless you give him six months," said Alpha. So the emphasis was on his son's preference, not on Lambda's needs nor the hospital's requirements. And here was the head of the department, steering the ship at the helm, making choices that suited his family and not the department, nor the patients. He was a big wig at the Guild of Surgeons. What an example he was setting!

"You first go for three months, and stay there until I am satisfied that you have had enough training." Alpha was final in his decision. So he was going on an unpaid open ended training stint, with no defined end points and no measurable outcomes. Possession was everything, they say. Once he lost grip on his job and went overseas, he would be at the mercy of Alpha. All the while he would be paying his employees, and incurring rent and other expenses. It made no sense whatsoever. How could he be so unreasonable? But Lambda had no choice.

Then came the shock. "Dr Alpha has declined to be your supervisor. You need to find another supervisor within two weeks or cease practice." He could not believe his eyes when he read the letter from the Medical Board. Alpha had not discussed this with him at all. What was he supposed to do now? Fall at Alpha's feet and beg for help? He might as well have told him there was no place for him in this town and ended the harassment once and for all. But sanctimonious men like Alpha did not operate like that. He would grind him to dust without appearing to do so.

"If I was your supervisor I would have to report on every small detail of your practice. That would not be in your interest. But I am still your mentor. I still support your endeavors to obtain this further training." Still it did not strike him as suspicious. How could a man of such high standing do underhand things? That would be unbecoming of a leader of the profession.

So the charade of "My son and I" "helping Lambda" continued. Lambda had to scramble to find another supervisor. Thankfully he found one. Perhaps Alpha expected him to leave at this point. He was probably dragging this out and playing for time until Junior was ready. But Lambda the naive starry eyed idealist still thought Alpha would, in the end, do what was morally and ethically right. And Alpha continued to smile and be polite. 'Why would he be nice to me if he was planning to install his son in my place all along?' thought Lambda.

Even on the day prior to his leaving for training Alpha was all smiles when he talked to him to hand over patients. Lambda felt reassured that everything was going to be alright.

That was the feeling when he left for his overseas training. But that was only the beginning of his travails. Once he left, Alpha and the medical director ceased all communication with him. The emails and telephone calls went unanswered. He was cut loose. He found himself banging his head against a brick wall.

So when he returned, Alpha had well and truly ensconced his own son in Lambda's position. It was a shock beyond belief. How could this man who was supposed to be one of the pillars of the Vascular Federation, do this mean thing. Righteousness says Job, is the only cloth that will cover one's nakedness when they go up to meet their maker. And here was a naked emperor strutting his obscene stuff openly in front of the world. And the world was silent. The world was witness to this dastardly act. Yet no one raised their voice. None. Zilch. Everyone at the hospital knew what had happened, that one career was killed so that another could thrive; yet no one deemed it fit to say anything. Anything at all.

He wrote to the authorities complaining about what happened. He wrote to them about the high amputation rates and the inordinately large number of synthetic graft implantation in dialysis surgery. But his pleas fell on deaf ears. He asked for whistle blower protection. But none was forthcoming. He was told that he was now an ex employee. Hence he could not blow the whistle. Yes the whistle was out of his reach!

And his bills kept mounting with unerring regularity. He continued to practise in the private sector. But the oxygen had been snuffed out of his practice. It was dying. He had hoped that someone would hear his pleas and give him justice. He was like an earthquake victim trapped under rubble. He was appealing to everyone. But no one seemed to be interested.

Undaunted he continued to practise. His vascular laboratory still produced world class exams. Even under financial pressure he refused to charge co payment from his patients. His patients loved him. His staff loved him. His faith that justice would be done one day was unshakeable. Truth shall set you free he had read. He was absolutely sure that truth would come out one day.

But the truth never came out. Instead, more lies came in the form of Alpha. When a patient of his was admitted to the public hospital with a complication, Alpha made an exaggerated complaint distorting facts and accusing him of abrogating the patient and falsifying medical records. Alpha had conducted a kangaroo court of his own, enlisted Beta and notified the Medical Board of his 'findings.' He had conveniently hidden the fact that Lambda no longer had admitting rights at the public hospital; and of course he had not revealed the fact that Lambda and he had had a long history. He had omitted the fact that Lambda's continued presence in town was an embarrassment for him and his son.

So that's what led to the suspension. And that is why he was here. He was trying to get help from everyone he could think of. The Guild of Surgeons was the epitome of excellence in surgery. If he could not complain to them, who else could he complain to? The politicians seem to be uninterested. The regulators seemed to be prejudiced. At least the Guild, the last word in matters surgical, should do something. Justice had to be done.

It was a long story. Perhaps he should not have allowed this to go on this long. Had he done something earlier, it would have been much easier to explain to the onlookers what happened. But the complex web of intrigue and deception spun around him by Alpha had totally disarmed him until he was in the middle of this abyss. Hindsight is 20/20 they say. But even in hindsight he was confused. What really happened? Surely this was happening to other people too? How could all these be hidden. How could bullies and nepotizers thrive in the system without scrutiny. Those who knew how to play the system escaped scot free. It was a shameful order he was living under. But he was powerless to change anything.

Chapter 11

"**W**hat do you expect us to do?" asked the Bullying Czar. She had sat through his monologue without uttering a word. When she thought he had finished, she broke the silence.

"Did you take in all I said?" asked Lambda. He was visibly upset after going through his traumatic experience. He could not stop a tear forming in the corner of his left eye. He turned quickly trying to hide it from her. He took a tissue from the box and pretending to blow his nose but surreptitiously wiped his tear. Men don't cry. It was a sign of weakness. He did not want her to see him at his most vulnerable state.

"There is a lot of hay fever these days." She pushed the box of tissues towards him. She had a sympathetic smile on. Whatever her inner thoughts were, this outward show of understanding put him at ease. At least she did not revel in his weakness.

"You need to act to stop this bullying!" said Lambda.

"We define the terms bullying, harassment and sexual harassment in a strictly legal way. I am not sure if any of the incidents you describe fit into this."

She was correct. The legal definitions may not fit exactly what he was subjected to. But surely this was harassment. This was workplace mobbing. This was collusion. He needed justice.

"If this is not bullying what is bullying?" he asked in exasperation, his hands turned up in a gesture towards the heavens. "No one calls you the N word or paki; no one directly approaches you for sex; no one tries to grab you. Those days are long gone. Bullying is alive and kicking and it is very subtle. Surely what happened to me was not normal. And the fact that the boss's son replaced me stinks badly. There must be a legal remedy for this!" he said.

"I am an employee of the Guild. I am bound by the remit given to me by my employer. I understand where you are coming from. There are many others in your situation. Everyone feels that they have been wronged. But we are unable to intervene."

Her answer was final. He had come all the way to another city to hear this. He was a fool. He had wasted precious funds on this non productive activity, just as he had wasted his money going on a wild goose chase called further training arranged by Alpha. How naive had he been? He never learned from his mistakes. To expect justice from this close knit Mafia juggernaut was very stupid indeed.

But his main characteristic was tenacity. When the adversity increased, his resistance too increased correspondingly.

"I am not going to take no for an answer from you. Have you had legal advice?" he persisted, hoping to escalate the matter until someone saw his point of view.

"Well if you want to meet our lawyer we can try to get an appointment with him. I cannot guarantee that he will see you today. But I will see what we can do."

She did show some empathy. He had come all the way from another city. She wanted him to finish his business on the same day. She left him in her office and went somewhere. Her assistant offered him another cup of coffee which he gratefully accepted. After all it was subscription from him and other members like him that was financing all this hospitality, he thought. But they were just employees. They did not know the politics behind all this. They were just being nice, as one human being would be to another.

The Bullying lady returned in a short while. "You are lucky our lawyer is in office today. He has kindly agreed to see you in two hours time. Why don't you go out and enjoy our beautiful city, and return in two hours. Come to my office and I will take you there."

He used this recess to have a stroll around the beautiful park laden city center. The Guild was right in the middle of the city on prime real estate. Its sprawling buildings seemed to mock him. This Guild was built on the success of the powerful surgeons. But for each man who built his fiefdom in his field there were several victims like you who were sacrificed. We were built on the ashes of the careers of hundreds of blooming surgeons, they seemed to tell him. His career may have been up in smoke but the invoices and subscription notices continued to pursue him like the taxman. It is a make believe empire, far removed from the patients, he thought.

When he returned she was waiting for him. "Come with me," she said taking him through one long corridor after another. Finally they arrived at the corporate legal office. It was called 'Risk Management Center.' Managing what risk and for whose benefit, he thought. Certainly not for the patients.

She must have read his thoughts. "We are a big entity. We have lots of assets and we employ many people. We need to save ourselves from law suits." Again the department had multiplied with many junior lawyers working under the suzerainty of a few seniors. Then they had assistants and secretaries. This was all paid for by our subscriptions he thought. Indirectly the cost for this extravagance would be passed on to the consumers. Perhaps he would have thought differently if he was on the other side of the fence. Now he was a renegade. And the full force of the establishment was against him. Whether he liked it or not he was in the ring and he had to fight.

The chief lawyer, or the risk management guru, was a smartly dressed suave man in his forties. He wore bow tie, a status symbol within the Guild. Did he have connections to get in, thought Lambda.

"Can you explain to me how and why the Guild needs to be involved?" asked the dapper man as he peered into Lambda's eyes. The complaints lady took leave at this point. She did not want to hear the sop story all over again. A loser's tale of woe is boring. No one wants to hear it twice.

But for Lambda the trauma began all over again as he relived the painful emotions once more, telling the story to this new man. As he repeated his tale, his mind started to block out some of the minutiae as it tried to protect itself from plunging into the depths of depression once more.

"Ok I understand exactly how you feel'" said the man in bow tie. It was a lie. How could he, from the upper crust of a privileged elite, even begin to comprehend the loss that Lambda felt, of losing the career that he had painfully built over years of struggle and sacrifice? But he had to say that. He had been to communication courses and he knew the importance of reflection. His poker face did not show any emotion though his mouth uttered words of comfort.

After a pause that seemed to stretch never endingly, the lawyer explained his position. "The issues you raise relate to employment. You need to raise that with your employer. We cannot be involved in that."

"Hang on! The Guild is involved deeply in every aspect of a surgeon's life. They organized the so called "Review!" How can you simply wash you hands off this?" interjected Lambda.

"Let me finish! I don't appreciate you interrupting when I speak. My trail of thought will be lost." This time he looked at Lambda sternly. He would put this interloper in his place.

"The issue about performance is something you have to take up with the medical regulators. The Guild can do nothing about it once the issue has gone to that level." He continued. "Though I sympathize with your situation I can do nothing to help you!"

"The Guild sends a nominee to all the appointments committees when they appoint surgeons to the public system." Lambda tried to justify why the Guild should be involved. But he knew he was fast losing ground. The voice was weak. He was no match for a seasoned lawyer when it came to debating skills.

"That is correct. We need to maintain standards. We are there to ensure that the appointees are either members of the Guild, or are of equivalent standard." After another pause he continued "We are there as observers. We do not tell them whom to select. We tell them whom not to select. This has been the tradition. We ensure that the surgical standards are maintained."

There was another pause. The bow tie man had really mastered the art of pausing for effect. When he finally uttered his words in a measured tone they had much more impact than if he had been talking free style.

His argument had lost its wind. Lambda was no match for this seasoned debater. He quickly moved onto the next topic.

"You say you cannot interfere with what the medical regulators do. But it was the report of the Guild of Surgeons which started this whole process. They kept changing the terms of reference. Even so, one of the clauses was that the review would be stopped and the Medical Board informed, should they find anything dangerous. They completed the review which means they did not find anything dangerous. Yet the review was sent to the Medical Board with numerous factual errors. It was sent as the Guild review. There was no natural justice. The cases that were reviewed have not been discussed at local level or externally, with my participation, several years on. And you say you cannot be held responsible!"

Lambda poured his heart out. He was not well versed in the art of pausing and using fewer words. He was emotional. But this got him nowhere. Heart to heart talks are for losers. Winners know how to spin and twist the words and stump their opponents. Besides, it would be possible to wake up somebody who was truly asleep. But it would be impossible to arouse someone who was pretending to sleep. When the hearts were hard and the minds were closed, no amount of pleading would change anything. This was a world of winners. The losers were allowed to exist out of kindness of heart. But they were not important.

"Since you are talking about surgical standards I would ask you to meet the Director of Standards. I am not a doctor. I look after legal matters only. From what you say you have no locus standi. That's all that I look after. You will have no cause to bring a lawsuit against us."

Looking intently at Lambda he said "One small piece of advice: do not fight the Guild. The Guild is very powerful. You are either one of us, or you are nobody if you want to practise surgery in this country."

Having said this he called the complaints lady's extension and asked her to arrange for Lambda to meet the Director of Standards.

"No one is taking ownership of my problem. Where do I go when the Gods of Surgery turn a blind eye?" asked Lambda as he got up from his chair. He added "Thank you any way."

"You are most welcome." The bow tie man smiled sarcastically. He added "We don't own you. We don't own your problems. You need to solve them yourself."

Thus ended another meeting with a stone. The complaints lady came in twenty minutes, as Lambda waited outside the lawyer's office.

As she took him back to her office she asked in a sympathetic tone "Did you have any joy with him?"

"No!" was Lambda's terse reply.

"I thought so. He is very tough. And you don't have a case against us."
She added "Why do you want to see the Director of Standards? I can easily see what his answer would be."

"I still want to see him. If nobody tells him what is happening he would think everything is hunky dory in his empire."

"As you wish. If you want to meet him I will try to arrange an appointment. He is a busy man."

As it turned out the Director of Standards was not available that day. Lambda had to make a choice. Having come all the way from another city he did not want to leave any stone unturned. Yes they were stones, literally. But he had to do what he had to do. He would not forgive himself for not trying hard enough, if he chose expedience and just caught the flight back home that night. He had already lost a lot of money. Spending a bit more on changing his flight and booking a night's accommodation was not going to alter his burgeoning expenses significantly. He settled for the appointment at eleven in the morning the following day.

The rest of the day went very slowly for Lambda. Just as he had trusted Alpha to do what was fair and righteous, he had trusted the Guild to do what was right. He did not know the legalities of his situation but he knew that he had been subjected to constructive dismissal and that he was wrongfully deprived of his employment. He had pinned a lot of hope that the Guild would take up his cause and would fight for him. He had pinned so much hope on this trip to the Guild head quarters. It was like he came on a pilgrimage to the Gods of Surgery asking for relief. But he got none. As the day progressed he understood that the emphasis was on passing the buck and avoiding legal responsibility. The Guild wanted the right to control a surgeon's life. But with the rights came the responsibilities, which everyone seemed to be shrugging off.

He knew that tomorrow would be the same. Same old repetition of Guild policies and excuses. He was looking at a very dark future. The one ray of hope he had had been snuffed out.

When he turned up at the Mecca of Surgery the next day he was directed to the Director of Standards. A balding man in a grey suit, this director too wore a bow tie, the symbol of belonging in this elite club. He was a retired surgeon. Well this was a great way to retire. This is a fantastic superannuation plan, thought Lambda. Not only that, he had power over life and death of surgeons.

The chubby man was quite pleasant. He could afford to be. When power comes without accountability who would not be.

"Welcome to your home, Dr Lambda," he smiled. "What can I do for you?"

This fucker has the gumption to ask this, thought Lambda! After all it was the Director of Standards who advised the hospital to organize the external review. He knew what was happening. But he pretended not to.

Lambda had no other option but to repeat the sad story, reliving the trauma for the third time in twenty four hours. It was torture. His voice quivered as he spoke. His mind tended to black out some events. Was he losing his memory? In any case he managed to tell his version of events.

The Director was looking at his watch on and off. "I have an appointment to go to in half an hour. So please tell me what we should do."

When one is rushed and hassled the performance suffers. All the rehearsed speech that he had prepared overnight vanished from his mind. Lambda had thought block after thought block. And his presentation came to a stuttered close.

"Once again tell me how we can help." His adversary was looking at him in the eye and telling him to hurry up as he had other important matters.

"You can withdraw the Guild report for starters." Lambda gathered himself and honed in on the one thing that had started all the mayhem in his life.

"What do you mean Guild report, and why should it be withdrawn?" The man with the bow tie feigned surprise and raised his arms with upturned palms in a gesture that seemed to be telling him 'I know nothing about what you are talking about.'

"The report that started it all; the draft report that gave me no chance to reply; the report that had so many factual errors that one would question the competence of the reviewers; the report that emanated from the ganged up slugfest against me by a few carefully hand picked staff; the report that stalled my career." Pausing for a moment he said "Furthermore, the report one of the authors of which was fired from his job for sexual harassment subsequently!"His emotions were at bursting point. He thought when one of the reviewers was found to be of inadequate moral standard, the whole report would lack credibility.

"That report was not a Guild report!"

This was a shocker.

"Then what was it? The Medical Board keeps calling it the "Guild of Surgeons Report." By attaching its name to the report the Guild has given it a lot of weight and carry. It gives a kind of official aura to it."

"But that is their perception. I tell you categorically now that it was not a Guild report." He was fiddling with his bow tie. But he stuck to his guns.

"Whose report is it in that case? You arranged the review."

"No I didn't. The hospital wanted to investigate your practice. All that the Guild did was to facilitate the investigation. We suggested two of our members to the hospital, which they accepted. This was actually to help you. You don't want any Tom, Dick and Harry to review your practice do you? So we have a pool of reviewers among our members whom we suggest. This is to maintain the standards of the review. Beyond this we have no involvement. It was a hospital review and if you have a problem with that you should raise it with the hospital!"

"Well the hospital already sent it to the Medical Board without any input from my end, and including all the factual errors. So where do I get justice?"

"The hospital is responsible. Not us," said the director, digging his heels in.

He would not budge from his position. "So the Guild suggests the names of the reviewers; the Guild is involved in drawing the terms of reference; two of the Guild members conduct the review; they use the Guild framework of competencies; they correspond on the Guild letterhead. And yet the Guild is not accountable for their actions? It is like if a Macdonald's franchise starts serving substandard food and chicken tikka masala, you cannot complain to the Macdonald's head quarters!"

"We are not a franchise and we are not a food shop. Your analogue is wrong. We just help the hospitals to maintain the standards." Holier than thou, he was saying.

"So you are not interested in maintaining the standards of the review? You will not entertain feed back about the reviewers? Will you use the same reviewers in the future in spite of my complaint about their competence?" Lambda's face was red with anger. His hands were trembling. He was fast losing the control that he had maintained with so much difficulty until then in his current sojourn in the quest for justice.

"Sorry I have to go now. Good to have met you. All the best." The Director stood up and extended his right hand towards Lambda. This was exactly what the reviewers had done at the first visit. They had a flight to catch. And they had to check the sports scores. They did not have any time for Lambda.

He lost it. He lost his cool demeanor and composure which he had maintained admirably thus far in this trip.

"This is unbelievable. This is fucking ridiculous! You control the selection for training, you control the content of training, you control the exams, you control the reviews, and indirectly control the medical regulation. Aren't you a cartel? What is the difference between El Chapo and you?"

Lambda screamed in anguish, and hit the table with his fists as he got up.

"Shhh! Respect! That is the key word. We operate with respect. You swore at me. You hit my table. You got up in a threatening manner. I can call in the security and get you thrown out. I can even get you arrested for verbal abuse and threatening behavior. Imagine a criminal conviction on top of all your problems? I can send you to the fucking jail."

All his gentle veneer had gone. Now he was staring at Lambda with sheer hatred and anger. He was breathing rapidly. His eyes flamed. In fact he was now using the power vested on him directly. Until then he was a part of a charade that maintained a surface of civility to the power games that the elite indulged in. Now he was exercising the power in its stark and naked form. He was using the power vested on him by the membership, indirectly by the public. Yes his power emanated from the people. But here he was, relishing his ability to put down this loser.

"Now be a good boy and go back to where you came from. I have explained to you enough!"

When he was reluctant to step out the bow tied gentleman took a step towards him. Waving a finger in his face menacingly he said "Now clear out of my office."

That brought his pilgrimage to a closure. The Gods of Surgery were not smiling. Well he should have known. They were all friends of Alpha. Lambda was a rank outsider!

Chapter 12

Arriving back in Big Smoke he was feeling extremely lonely and down. He needed Gamma next to him now more than ever. He needed someone in whom he could confide and discuss all his problems, frailties and disappointments. But she was not scheduled to meet him for a few days yet. He had downed a couple of glasses of gin and tonic on the flight. This had helped him to forget about his current situation and sleep during the flight. Then the train journey. It was close to midnight when he reached home. He was tired. He just crashed on the bed.

It was well past sunrise the next day when he woke up. He was an early riser. So this was unusual for him. But it didn't matter. It was not like he had to wake up and get ready for work. He was newly unemployed. He had an appointment with his solicitor in Big Smoke in three days time. That was all he had for the rest of the week. It didn't matter if he slept the whole day or not. This was unusual for him. He was usually driven by targets. Every day he would plan his diary as soon as he woke up. He was not used to sitting around on his hands doing nothing. What a waste of trained manpower for the community? But no one seemed to care. The Guild of Surgeons was all powerful. And the politicians and regulators appeared to toe its line without too much fuss.

Until his visit to the Guild head quarters he was hopeful that he would get help from them; that they would help him get out of the morass that he found himself in. As long as he had that hope he could cope. But that was gone now.

And he did not realize how much he would miss Gamma. He had known her only for a short time. But within this short while he had begun to like her a lot. And he began craving for her company. Was he falling in love? No, he said to himself. He was in deep shit. He did not want to encumber another human being with all his problems. Yes she was a good friend. That that was all there was to it. He could not start a relationship at this point.

He was spreading butter on his bread when his phone rang. Who would look for him? He was an unwanted unemployed person. Who on earth would want to talk to him?

"How did it go?" It was Gamma. That was a pleasant surprise. "I thought you are doing a program or something. Are you back in Big Smoke now?" He couldn't hide his happiness. He was really really happy to hear her voice.

"Something happened. So I cut short my trip and returned last night. I can't explain over the phone. Tell me what happened to you?"

She too sounded eager to talk to him. She was one soul that had not judged him, and treated him with affection and respect. "Nothing new. In any case I too don't want to discuss things on the phone. Why don't we meet?"

"Sounds like a plan. Why don't you come to my place. Let's talk," she said. He knew that if he went to her place they would end up doing a lot more than just talk. But her voice did not betray any eagerness or anticipation. Something is amiss thought he.

He couldn't wait to meet her. They hugged and slowly kissed. Once they were comfortably settled on the couch she asked "Shall I fix you a drink." He thankfully accepted. He may have to drive home later but now he needed a drink. She made him a Bourbon.

"You tell me about your adventure first. Then I will tell you about mine. Not an adventure really but the reason for coming back early." She seemed somewhat preoccupied with something. But she wasn't giving away much.

"Well my mission was a total failure. They are not interested in going against one of their own." He briefly explained to he what had happened at his three meetings. Finally he confessed that he was thrown out by the Director of Standards. It took a lot for him to admit to a woman that he had been shown the door by a man. But he swallowed his pride and truthfully narrated everything to her.

"To be perfectly honest I expected this. Do you think birds of a feather will not flock together? They have been playing this game for decades. They are well and truly entrenched. Do you think an interloper like you can shake their bonds apart? I am sorry but you are naive my friend."

She was more street smart than him. His quest for righteousness and justice had come a cropper. Now this did not surprise her.

"The only route open to you is the legal route. The law may grind slowly but if we work hard and prove our innocence we can win."

"Why do you say we?" He did not want her to waste her brilliant career for his sake. He did not deserve it.

"As a friend I cannot stand by and watch them do this to you. If you trust me, please take me with you when you meet your lawyer. But don't think we are in a relationship. I need to sort out some things in my life before I can think of any commitment."

He appreciated her honesty. "Now tell me what is going on in your life. Why did you come back early?"

"You missed something!" she said with a smile.

"What did I miss?" He was puzzled.

"My primary doctor found a small lump in my right breast. It was during a routine physical!"

"Hey I did not look at you as a patient!" he protested. He was genuinely concerned. "When is the biopsy? Hope it is not malignant?"

"I am seeing a breast surgeon tomorrow. I will let you know after that. Funny these breast lumps. I had a mammogram six months ago and there was nothing!" She did not want to involve him in her problems. On the contrary she wanted to help him regain his licence and get back to his normal work. She did not want a career to end just because the head of the department had a sinister plan.

"I sincerely hope this is a benign lump. But please don't neglect this. Do what you have to do. That is far more important than my career. Life before career. I want you to live long."

Both of them held hands and remained silent for a long time. "I am sorry we are starting wrong footed. But adversity should bring out the best in both of us," she said as he took leave for the night. They were not in a mood for any physical activity but she insisted that he had his dinner before he left.

He could not accompany her for her doctor's visits. Her sister came from another state to be with her. She did not want the paparazzi to get wind of her health problems. Nor did she want them to suspect she had a new man in her life. That would set them off on a hunt for information on him. That in turn, would attract adverse publicity for him.

But she insisted that she accompanied him to meet his lawyer. He was actually grateful for that. Two brains were always better than one. And she appeared to have more common sense than his lofty idealistic and naive mind. But secrecy was paramount. She had her dress code when she went on secret missions. The burqa had helped her on many previous occasions. It was her trusted friend.

His lawyer did not object when he asked if he could bring a friend.

"Wow! I did not know that you had an Islamic lady friend!" His lawyer was impressed. He was a humanist. He did not believe in parochial boundaries. He was glad that his client had similar values.

That was until she removed her burqa. "Oh you!" he exclaimed. He was one of Gamma's numerous fans. "What do we owe this VIP visit for?"

"I am just here in the capacity of a friend. My friend Lambda needs all the help we can muster. I have contacts in many places. I can help unearth useful information, you know."

The lawyer was unimpressed. "Information like what?" he asked, in a surprised tone.

"Well we are trying to save a career. We need to explore all angles. For example what if Alpha had an affair with the nursing sister who led the mobbing of Lambda. Will it help?"

"Sure it will. It is going to be like Donald Trump's Russia investigation! Even if he waved facing Moscow that would become a news story." He smiled. He was happy that a TV personality was taking an interest in his client's case.

After the preliminaries they agreed on a specific time to work out the details.

Chapter 13

They arrived early for the case conference. In fact they had arrived before the lawyer's secretary, which meant they had to wait outside the office. It was situated in a multi storey building in a posh corner of the city. They had to park in an adjacent public park and had to walk through tunnels and connecting corridors to arrive at their destination. This meant they would be seen together. Nobody knew Lambda. But Gamma was well known. It was not that she did not want to be seen near a legal office. That would be quite normal for a career woman. She was not going to see a psychologist, after all. But she just did not want to be seen with Lambda. Not with any man for that matter. Not at this stage. She did not want any scandals to break out that would distract their attention. They had two priorities. Firstly to clear Lambda's name. Secondly she had to deal with her health scare.

She had extracted a promise from him that he would not ask any questions about her health until his problem was over. She did not want him to worry about her. His body mind and soul should be focused on only one thing: on clearing his name. His name was more important to him than his life. And she too recognized this. There was no room for personal emotions at this time. Besides, she did not want him to be too involved in her affairs until she was sure she would not cause him any more stress. She was helping him without any expectations. But it certainly benefited her by taking her mind away from her own problems.

As usual she adhered to her dress code for such occasions: burqa and shades. It gave her the feeling of security. "Looks like we are early," said Lambda. "Shall we have some coffee?"

"I am not going to sit in a cafe with you, at least for now. You can bring me a cup of cappuccino," she smiled. He walked to the next block to get her a cuppa as well as the usual black coffee for himself. The streets thronged with people going to their work places or businesses. Hmm! He would have been busy like them had not Alpha ambushed him. But what was the point in crying over spilt milk? He had to work on what needed to be done.

By the time he returned to the office Mr. Theta had arrived, along with his secretary and the receptionist. "Good morning. I am sorry I am late. The trains are very unreliable these days." he beamed, as he ushered them in. "We could have made you the coffee. Next time I promise we will be waiting for you with coffee."

He was a very friendly. He was tall and well built. He had a middle age paunch and a receding hairline with a salt and pepper appearance in the remaining hair. He could have been a basketball player or a soccerite in his previous birth. But now his sedentary life and career worries had taken their toll. He was one of the few independent lawyers in the city who had not joined a conglomerate. He lived about an hour away by train. Free of the hassle of driving and parking in the city he was able to get a lot of his work done during the commute. The trains had wifi access too which meant he had a head start to the day, having cleared the overnight freight of emails while still in the train.

"Make yourselves comfortable. Today's session is just to plan our strategy. We will not get to the nuts and bolts of the individual cases today. But in a sense today's decisions are the most important ones you will make in the present situation. I do not want to rush you. I have set aside the whole morning for you. I have to be at a hearing at one o'clock in the afternoon. But we have the whole morning to ourselves."

Once they had had a chance to have their beverage, he came into the room they were seated in, with a note pad and a pen. "I am still old fashioned. I could never get used to ipads and other electronic devices. Nothing like old pen and paper," he said as he sat in the couch next to Gamma. "I will have to call my secretary to take notes at certain points. But we can get started without her."

He continued, looking at Lambda. "Doctor I have to tell you that you are in a very difficult situation. Rightly or wrongly you have allowed yourself to be led into a tight corner. Your adversary is not only formidable in terms of power, he is also very intelligent and cunning. He has played you like a fiddle. You are not even close to realizing how badly he has stitched you up."

"Well, truth has to triumph!" said Lambda, with a firm resolve. "He may be formidable. He may have friends in high places. But God is mightier than the mightiest man. I know we are in a David versus Goliath situation. But I am very confident that justice will be done." Lambda was adamant that he would win this battle for his career.

"I applaud your self belief and belief in justice and truth. But unfortunately truth doesn't always win. It is your word against his. And his word carries a lot more clout!" The lawyer was realistic.

"Before we start I have to warn you about one thing. I don't need to know if you are telling the truth or not, but you have to remember everything you say. Once you have put your version out there you cannot take it back. That means if you contradict yourself on a future occasion you will be mince meat in the hands of the opposing barrister. This is a game and if we play the game according to the rules, we may be able to win, or at the very least, limit the damage."

"If you tell the truth at all times, you don't have to remember what you said." Lambda was defiant, as he tried to remember whether it was Nelson Mandela or Confucius who said that.

"It is good to be idealistic. But truth has many shades. It is an art to tell some thing that is not a lie but not the total truth either. Unfortunately those who master this, will win. Others will not," he continued. "This is a wicked world. The medical regulation industry in this country is draconian. It is a self serving field. If the regulators don't have anything to do, they will cease to have a reason to exist. And a whole lot of other people, myself included, will lose their jobs. And when something happens due to their failure to act, the press will roast them alive. On the other hand if they take harsh action more than what is necessary, no one will suffer, except the doctor and his staff and family. To be really cynical, when the Board takes action it creates a lot of activity. It keeps us in business."

"And the government wonders where the health care dollars are going!" interjected Gamma, who had been silently observing the conversation.

"The moment you become the health minister I will close shop and leave town. But jokes apart I am your lawyer and I am hundred percent committed to getting you out of this mess." Mr. Theta was a kind man, in spite of years of being in an unforgiving profession, where playing hard and playing to win were considered virtues.

"You have two options. The Medical Board's decision can be challenged in court; or you can appeal to the Board to review their decision, saying there is new information that they need to consider."

"We can't appeal to the same people. They are biased. Especially Dr Vector!" Lambda raised his voice in spite of trying to keep his cool.

"Calm down; calm down! Unless you have definitive proof that Dr Vector acted in bad faith, you cannot say that!" Mr. Theta still believed appealing to the Medical Board was the option with the best chance to succeed.

"I will explain why. When a doctor has been totally banned or suspended, as in your case, the Courts will either rule to lift the ban or to keep it. It is an all or none decision. There is no half way house. The courts have no power to impose conditions on your licence. On the other hand, if you had not been suspended, and only conditions had been imposed on your license, the courts could make an order to vary the conditions, if they are unfair conditions. As you can see the courts are reluctant to lift the ban on any doctor whose competence has been questioned.

"Dumb as it sounds, the Board can lift their ban and impose conditional licensing. But not the courts. The law is an ass here. And I know that on the few occasions that the courts did lift the ban on a doctor, the Medical Board has hurriedly convened to impose impossible conditions so that the doctor cannot practise any way. It is a power game. And they don't like their authority to be challenged."

"I can't go back to them. They are biased. It is too traumatic to sit across the table from Dr Vector who has already made up his mind!"

"I can only give you my honest professional opinion. But I will do whatever you instruct me to do," said Theta.

There was an awkward silence in the room. Finally Gamma spoke: "What if there were procedural errors in the original hearing?"

"Then it is a no brainer. If they have made a procedural error that has potentially prejudiced the outcome of the Medical Board hearing, the courts will throw out their decision without a second thought. And the Board will have no leg to stand on. Which means they will not reconvene to impose further sanctions on you."

"Didn't you tell me that Dr Vector is a member of Alpha's organization?" asked Gamma, looking pleadingly at Lambda. She desperately wanted a legal point on which the entire decision to suspend Lambda could be overturned. That was the only way his honor could be restored. Pleading to the Board to impose conditions would be accepting that he was in the wrong.

"Yes, Dr Vector is a member of the organization of which Dr Alpha is the president!" screamed Lambda. "There is an obvious conflict of interest! And this was not declared." Perhaps they had stumbled upon the one legal point that could completely demolish the Board's credibility.

"Please don't get carried away. We are all members of one organization or another. How can you say that there was a conflict of interest when you cannot prove that Dr. Vector had a pecuniary or other gain due to him being a member of the organization of which Dr Alpha is president? For example I am a member of the United Mileage Plus frequent flier program. If the CEO of United Airlines makes a complaint about something, and I am in the judgment panel, should I have to declare that?" Pausing a while, he said "I would probably declare it but others may feel differently about this!" Mr. Theta was pensive.

"What if I tell you that the Vascular Federation of which Alpha is the president and Vector is a member, fights for vascular surgeon reimbursements? In fact they have a separate committee that deals with coding etc. which lobbies the politicians with a view to maximize vascular surgeons' income. In other words Vector's income has been increased by at least one dollar due to the efforts of the Federation!"

"Hmmm! That is interesting. You may be onto something there!" Mr. Theta knew he was talking to someone who was highly intelligent.

"But you told me that the Vascular Federation is responsible for the selection of trainees, the curriculum, the training and assessment of the trainees as well as the exams?" Gamma was skeptical.

"Yes, they do all that and also recommend to the minister the people who could serve on regulatory bodies. Furthermore the Guild of Surgeons, of which the Federation is an integral part, also control the medical experts who give medico legal opinion about surgeons, and all other aspects of a surgeon's life! They are like the Hindu Trinity of Gods, Brahma, Vishnu and Shiva who preside over creation, preservation and destruction of the world!"

"You mean to say the Commerce Commission allows this? This is anti trust. It is a cartel! There is no two words about that!" Mr. Theta was surprised no one had raised this in the course of his long career.

"It is a Mafia. Alpha is the boss, and Vector is an undeclared member!" smiled Lambda.

"It is not enough to just show that Vector did not declare his conflict of interest. It will be much stronger if you could show some evidence that they had communicated close to the hearing. That will make his position untenable." Mr. Theta wanted a waterproof case before deciding to take the punt of going to the courts rather than appeal to the Board.

"How can I prove that they talked to each other? I am not FBI!" Lambda did not know where to turn to.

"Think hard. Was there any meeting of the Federation or some occasion where they might have met?" asked Gamma, hoping to jog his memory.

"There was one but Vector did not attend as I saw his name in the list of apologies. I did not go either!"

"Think, doctor. Anything else?" Theta's enthusiasm was rapidly dwindling.

"Oh I went for a job interview about a month before the hearing. Vector was the head of the department in that hospital. The moment he saw me he excused himself out of the panel, which was strange. I had no idea that a complaint was brewing at that stage, but the incident had already happened about which Alpha complained, dealing the final fatal blow to my career."

"Hey don't say fatal blow. We are going to resurrect you like a Phoenix," interrupted Gamma.

"Ok, whatever the case may be. There were only two candidates shortlisted, and it was in an area of surgery where I had expertise. I was very hopeful that if I secured that job I could slowly wind down my office, as the former was a full time salaried position. But after a few weeks I got a letter saying I was unsuccessful, which irked me a lot. The letter went on to say they did not select anyone. I suspect Vector would have called up Alpha, though I did not name Alpha as one of my referees."

The pain of losing that opportunity was written all over his face as he sighed. "Had I got that job, I would have left town, and Alpha and his son could have lived happily ever after!"

"Most problems in life are created by greed and the craving for vengeance. So Alpha lost the opportunity to solve the issue amicably. He could have lived and let live." Mr. Theta had seen many instances like this in his career. "The Hippocratic oath was really a hypocrite's oath in the current day environment. "

"I am fighting not because I want to take revenge. I want justice!" said Lambda.

"I understand. I did not mean, you. Coming back to the interview if the panel had selected you and the job was denied to you because of a telephone conversation with Alpha, Vector should have documented it in the selection committee's file. If he had prior knowledge of the incident from the complainant before the complaint was actually lodged, he should not have sat on the panel inquiring into that complaint. He should have declared this and you should have been told about this."

Just then there was a call on his mobile phone. Theta excused himself and went into another room. He returned after five minutes.

"I am afraid we have to stop there for now. I need to help another doctor urgently. They are going to terminate his contract abruptly, another constructive dismissal! Unfortunately this is becoming all too common in this country. People want to build empires by destroying competition! He wants me to get an interim injunction in the courts."

"Could I have got an injunction when my contract was not renewed?"

"You could have. That is exactly what I would have advised you to do if you had come to me at that time. But Alpha was clever. He completely disarmed you by pretending to help. It was like getting the clothes off a woman by just sweet talking, before she even realizes that she is being stripped. I am sorry it is too late to rectify that. Let's concentrate on the present."

Asking them to make an appointment with his secretary, he summarized their discussions for the day. "So we agree to lodge a case in the courts. We need to work on getting the information about any possible contact between Alpha and Vector, such as call logs, files of the appointments committee and so on."

"Now that you are talking about call logs, I remember distinctly that Vector was staring at his iphone often, and was playing with it all the time during the hearing!" said Lambda.

"He may have been on call," said Gamma, trying to play down this line of thinking. "Are you suggesting that Vector was in contact with Alpha by texting during the trial? That is outrageous!"

"Even if he was on call he should have asked another doctor to cover for him. He should not have brought his phone into the room, period. Doing so is doing a grave injustice to you. Even if he did not communicate with Alpha, looking at the phone would have distracted him. He cannot do that when dealing with the career of a doctor!" Theta was emphatic on this. He continued, "Proving that Vector did not declare a conflict of interest is only one part of the equation. Our defense should be multipronged. We need to get expert witnesses who could testify on your behalf!"

"Experts to testify against Alpha? He is the president of the Federation!" said Lambda dejectedly. "It is a small community and they all stick together. Even if they express sympathy to me in private, they will not be willing to front up to Alpha in a court of law!"

"Well if no one in this country is willing we need to look afar, at international experts. In fact it is going to carry a lot more clout if your expert is internationally known. You need to help me by identifying potential persons of eminence in your field. Their practice should be contemporaneous. They should not be yesterday's men. Dinosaurs are regularly slayed in courts!"

"Also try to find out if there was any abnormal relationship between the two surgeons who undertook the original review, and Alpha. See if their report can be tainted. Who knows? One of them may become suddenly religious and repent and confess!"

"In fact one of them was fired for sexual misconduct!" said Lamda!

"I am going to send my pastor to meet them!" said Gamma.

"Don't forget Beta and the medical director. If any one of them should feel guilty and regret their actions, we have won the lottery," said Theta. He added, the complaint made by Alpha about you is disgraceful. He has made unsubstantiated attacks on your personal integrity, made highly exaggerated allegations, distorted facts and defamed you badly. In fact if he had made those statements outside you could have sued the hell out of him. But he has made these remarks under the pretext of notification. The law is draconian. It exempts anyone from being sued for notifications!" Theta paused for a moment before continuing. "But there is a code of conduct for doctors. It specifies how complaints against other medical practitioners should be made. At all times they should show respect!"

"Also he conducted his impromptu investigation without talking to me, came to his lopsided conclusions, and conveyed them in point form to the Medical Board, invoking his positions as president of the Federation, and as a senior examiner in the specialty. The Board were razzle dazzled by his report. They just presented to me his conclusions, ten in all but most of them repetitions of the same theme in one form or other, and asked for my answers. They had not taken the trouble to read and digest the facts to form their own opinion. I was completely stumped as I could not read his harangue and answer point by point. It was very unfair." Lambda was still smarting from the lack of procedural fairness.

"You need to make a counter complaint. You need to write to the Medical Board and the Guild of Surgeons, perhaps even to the Vascular Federation. He had no business to conduct his own inquiry without talking to you and without declaring his glaring conflict of interest vis-a-vis his son's appointment to the position previously held by you."

Theta continued, "I cannot make a complaint for you. But I can look over your draft unofficially. But remember, if you make a complaint it should list the specific instances in his complaint that violated specific provisions of the code of conduct."

"His complaint is one long confused jumble of allegations and more allegations. Where do I start and where do I finish? That was my problem during the hearing," said Lambda.

"It is easy. You need to be objective if you want to make an impact. Get different colored highlighter pens. Assign different colors to each type of violation. For example "Name calling or Vilification will be violet, Exaggeration will be yellow, and Falsehoods will be red, if I were to do it. Collusion could be green. Go through the entire document and mark each violation in color. Then list instances where each type of violation of the code occurred. It is hard work and it could take you a good few days. But in the end you will have a document of high quality that no one can ignore easily."

"Hey let me do it for you if you don't mind. I love coloring'" said Gamma.

With that their meeting came to an end.

"How am I going to repay your kindness?" asked Lambda as they got into his car.

"I am actually enjoying this. Until now it was all doom and gloom. But now is the fight back time. We have agreed upon certain leads. I love investigative journalism!" she smiled.

"But how can we get phone records?" asked Lambda. "Are you going to hack into their phones?"

"Phone records are easy. We can subpoena them through the courts. But the contents of the conversations are hard to prove, unless there were texts!"

She continued, "You have to understand that as journalists we have contacts in many places. We have hacking expertise available to us too."

"But Alpha and Vector would have erased all the chats in their phones!" Lambda was still very pessimistic about all this.

"No! All chats will be archived in the telephone providers. Besides regular chats we can look at Whatsapp, Facebook and other social media contacts too. If the aim is to prove that they had been in regular contact, and if this was indeed true, it is quite easy! This is the electronic age. Like Karma, your electronic footprint will follow you to the grave and beyond!"

"But why go to this extent to snoop into their affairs?"

"We are trying to save your career, remember? The career which you built up on so much hard work, sweat, blood and sacrifice! You can't stop a bus by running behind it. You need to get in front. You need to attack!"

Chapter 14

The drive back home was lonely for Lambda. After the high of meeting with Gamma and interacting with a highly intelligent lawyer which reminded him of the heady days when he pooled his brains with that of equally intelligent colleagues and juniors in attempting to treat patients, he was back to his dreary idle life. Those memories were from the days before he came to Alpha's unit. Here team work was something that you do once a year when you play a team sport in the annual juniors versus seniors matches. Yes, in Alpha's world, each man was for himself and Alpha the God was also for himself.

He called Gamma on the blue tooth. "Do you think I made a mistake by opting to go to the courts?" he asked.

"Absolutely not! Do you think you can appeal to the Board successfully?"

"If there were other people sitting on the panel I may be able to persuade them..." he dragged, leaving the sentence hanging.

"But you will get the same people! I don't know who selects the delegates and how. But allowing only two people to decide on your fate is an absolute disgrace. In other countries there will be a much larger and more representative panel deliberating before making such monumental decisions! But here you will get the same two when you appeal. And Dr Vector seems to be very much against you. The only way to overcome this is to go beyond them!"

She added, "Why do you think he is against you. Is it just his friendship with Alpha or is it because he is a racist?"

"I don't know what other 'ist' he is but he is a prejudist! He is prejudiced against me."

"But you have now found a way to get him off your back. Stick to your guns and he will be gone from your life in a tick. He will no longer be able to wave a life and death sword menacingly in your face!"

There was a pause. Then she said "Guess what I found when I came home! In my inbox there was an invitation from the Guild of Surgeons for our crew to attend a cocktail party. The occasion is the proclamation of the Bullying Charter. They want a lot of woman attendees to gain credibility. They say they are winning in the drive to get more women into surgical fields; they also want to acknowledge that there has been sexual harassment, bullying and discrimination in the past and say they have turned over a fresh leaf and have ended bullying from the profession!"

"Do you believe that?" asked Lambda. "Not after witnessing what happened to you! But I have decided to go. It will be in the city where they are head quartered. I will take a few weeks off after that and explore that city. I have spent too long in Big Smoke," she said.

"Are you hiding anything from me? Are you going to have treatment in that city?" he paused for a moment and then said "I have no right to ask. Who am I to you?"

"Come on, don't wallow in self pity. You are hugely important in my life. You are a friend. You have every right to ask. But I request you to please not ask about me until you finish your business. Don't be distracted! My problem is nothing compared to yours."

After a few seconds she asked "Are you there?"

"I am still online," he said.

"Don't think I have left you in the lurch. I have set two of our capable research assistants on your case. On the lines that we discussed. Please don't think I have forgotten those. With your permission I will liaise directly with Mr. Theta. You concentrate on getting medical experts and drafting the responses to the clinical issues raised by your villain. As for the coloring activity I have already started. I have almost run out of violet ink!"

"Ha ha has he vilified me so much?"

"Not just you. Others affiliated to you too. For example he says you "arranged" a job at the university and that is how you stayed in town even after you lost your appointment at the public hospital!"

"How can you just "arrange" a job at the university. Don't they have selection criteria and a vetting process? Arranging a job just like that, ah! My father must be the president of the university!"

"What was he thinking? He thinks nepotism or corruption is everywhere? Besides, how you stayed in town is immaterial to the complaint. By bringing this into the complaint he has betrayed his real motive which is to chase you out! What an idiot!"

"You can afford to be an idiot if you have connections in high places!" laughed Lambda just as his phone signal dropped. He was driving through the mountains. The call ended. He was apprehensive how he would spend the next several weeks. He had one person in his life to look forward to at that point in time. Now she was going incognito. How was he going to bear this separation? Was she hiding some bad news about her breast lump from him? The thought that she may have a serious illness was unbearable. It was even more hurtful than his own situation.

Chapter 15

The occasion was very intimidating. Lots of bow ties and high heels with wine glasses were strutting around. The heels made noises like a horse's trot each time the owner moved, from one bow tie to another, from one high heels to another. There was light banter. People were in good spirits, literally. Vintage wine and champagne were flowing like they were the rivers of like.

The place was the Guild of Surgeons building. The amazing architecture and high roofs provided an intimidating backdrop for the event. It was a meeting of the ancient and the modern. Ancient traditions trying to find relevance in a modern world. Change being the only constant those who did not change would perish. But this institution had resisted change for a long time. The hallowed precincts were also the witness to some of the worst abuses. Sexual discrimination, intimidation, racial discrimination and actual sexual abuse, had been perpetrated with the participation or acquiescence of those who occupied this building, for a long time.

Like a tyrannosaurus trying to adapt itself against the challenge of the mammals, this ancient institution was trying to rebrand itself. The traditional male rightwing machismo surgeon could not exist in the electronic era, at least in public. The scrutiny of the media was intense. The focus of the paparazzi had been on the Guild of Surgeons for some time, and the institution was fighting back in the only way it knew: more courses, more directorates, more people to handle complaints. And of course more propaganda. Today's gala event was part of this effort to redeem itself in the eyes of the public.

Gamma found herself surrounded by good looking men. Not only were they good looking, they were dapper in their black suits and bow ties. A few wore blazers and some wore ordinary neck ties. Most of the ties had the Guild insignia inscribed on them. The females too looked resplendent in formal suits or skirt and blouse. Many wore scarves. People were milling around chit chatting. Most knew each other. There was live jazz in the background.

Gamma was easily one of the most beautiful of the women. She wasn't dressed in formal attire. Some knew her while others had seen her face somewhere. They were wracking their brains trying to place this pretty chick. Who was she? And many vied for her attention.

The talk was mostly about their exploits. It was always ego driven. Listening to each, one could not but help think that person was the best surgeon in the world. Even the women there seemed to be driven by testosterone. Some of course were quieter. They were the silent soft power that women could bring to any team.

The men seemed to hone in on the women with feminine demeanor more than those who were boisterous and extroverted. Naturally Gamma was a star attraction.

"Ladies and Gentlemen! May I have your attention please?" called out a balding gentleman. He had golden robes on him. It was then that Gamma noticed a few robed gentlemen and some ladies among the crowd. Were they knights in Arthur's court? Or were they clowns who liked to dress themselves up? Whatever it may be the robes added to the ambience. This was a place of authority; of hierarchy; of strict social order.

The music stopped and they all paid attention. Conversations stopped half sentence. Such was the discipline of this group. In hushed silence everyone was waiting for their leader to utter the words he was expected to. In fact it had been circulated in the media, the text of what he was going to say.

"Today we have gathered to make an important announcement. We are entering a new era. An era of genuine respect for each other; an era of equal opportunity for men and women, and for gender neutral people; an era of equality for all people irrespective of color and creed."

Balderdash! thought Gamma. Does he really mean it? May be he will inspire the generations to come. But for those soaked in the traditional man dominated culture, will it make a difference? Were they all going to wake up tomorrow as new men and women? Will the traditions that had been inculcated into their souls be abandoned? Will they embrace the new culture with enthusiasm?

The gold robe laden leader carried on expounding the new order. There would be bullying courses online. Like halal certification, the budding surgeons would be bullying certified. Once certified, they would be bullying proof. That is, they would never bully anyone in their lives, leave alone careers. The bullying curriculum was carefully chosen. Some people had done doctorate in bullying. They were the pioneers in the bullying courses.

Then there was the hotline and the bullying department. They had recruited a full compliment of workers who would handle complaints, or rather, diffuse situations. As for punishment for the offenders, he chose to keep mum. "Lets hope we don't have to go there," he said.

There was thunderous applause. The leader had perhaps articulated what was a popular sentiment. There had been a paradigm shift in the surgeons' culture. That was what the world wanted to hear and the surgeons wanted the world to see and believe. Was this all a carefully stage managed drama? Can leopard change its stripes and zebra its spots?

Gamma's glass was refilled, probably at the prompt of the bow tie standing next to her now. A portly man with receding white hair, he had somehow edged the others to occupy the spot next to her. Was it his seniority or was it his cunning? He got what he wanted. He was one of the ruling elite. Could he be the man who threw out Lambda from his office, she wondered. But power does have attraction. And he was exuding power. Whether it was from the alcohol or his authoritative manner, he looked quite attractive to her.

Why am I thinking of him as being attractive? What is wrong with me, she wondered. She pinched herself to keep awake. The balding greying man with a paunch; but exuding power. His eyes were mesmerizing. But they kept darting between her cleavage and her face. She felt a strange exhilaration. His voice had a commanding ring to it. And the whole surrounding, the respect shown by others to this man, all played on her mind.

The main speaker had finished and many others took to the podium. The majority of the speakers were women, naturally. This event was to celebrate the ascension of women to equal status in the Guild. Like abolishing slavery, or reparations to the Maori by the Waitangi Tribunal, or the apology to the Aboriginals, this was a historic acknowledgement of a historic injustice. The press loved it. Though Gamma was part of the press invitees she was participating as an individual, having taken time off. It was nice to be able to absorb this momentous event without the pressure of having to report on it. She was enjoying it.

But did abolishment of slavery bring about equality for the blacks? Not for a hundred years. Even the civil rights movement a hundred years later may not have done it. Will this apology and policy change by the Guild really bring equal rights to women in surgery? Will it eliminate all forms of bullying? Or will it need another wave of indignation by the public at yet another case of appalling behavior to really make a difference at ground level?

"You are a TV girl aren't you?" the bow tied big man asked her. "Yes and no. Yes I belong to a network. But no I am not on duty," said Gamma, feeling uncomfortable on being called a girl. "Oh a non working TV girl! Non working women are a rare species these days. In the good old days we were the breadwinners and the women stayed at home, tending to the children. I suppose all good things have to come to an end!" he smiled.

"Well I am not a girl. Also we don't want to be treated as objects or maids at hand," said Gamma in a firm voice.

"Oh a defiant girl! I like them! It is always great to talk to one," he said. "I know, I know, I shouldn't be saying this. But whatever the Guild says, boys will be boys!" he winked.

Why didn't she feel angry or annoyed? It was as if some strange power had completely disarmed her defenses against this kind of behavior.

The last speech was going on in earnest. Some people had left. The big chief leaned over towards Gamma. "Are you booked for the night? We are having an after party. That is the time when we really let our hair down and be normal. Do you want to join us? This is a great opportunity to observe how the surgeons behave in private, when there is no public scrutiny or CCTV. Who knows, after seeing this you may want to marry a surgeon!"

"Why would I want to marry a surgeon?" asked Gamma.

"If you marry one you don't have to work ever again. He will earn and you can spend. When he gets tired of you he will give you half of his fortune. Then you will be a rich single woman!" he laughed at his own joke. Well only fools laugh at their own jokes. Wise people laugh at themselves; thought Gamma. But part of her wanted to see what the other side of the screen would be like. Surgeons without masks; that's how they operated in the eighteen hundreds. Then they surrounded themselves with layer after layer of procedures and protocols; They lost touch with reality.

She was curious to see how the surgeons would behave behind the scenes. She knew Lambda, well, quite intimately at that. But he was a loser. These surgeons were the winners. They were not only at the top of their game, they were also at the top of their society, perched in high places at the Guild. The bald eagles, she thought.

Though she wanted to say no, she found her mouth mumbling a feeble yes. Like a firefly going towards its nemesis she was attracted by the power, and the feeling of belonging to the "in" crowd.

This is wrong, she thought. She knew the other side of this power game. She had seen how the cartel-like behavior could destroy an honest well meaning surgeon's career. But she was also curious to see where this would lead to. She wanted to enjoy the second hand power play. She wanted to see what it would be like to bask in the glory of the powerful elite. What had come of her? Had she been pragmatic enough to give in to the advances of her television suitor she may have been flying high by now. She may have been dining with Rolls Royce and wining with bow ties. Had she missed the opportunity? What could have been? All she had for staying true to herself was misery and anxiety.

Her thought process was interrupted when the surgeon partner asked "We are going to a hotel. Would you like to ride with me in my Audi or my friend and wife, in their Merc?"

"I will go with you. But where is your wife?" she asked.

"She is at the races in another country. I had to delay my departure to attend this bloody event." He paused for a minute and continued "You know some idiot published something about a woman being asked for a blow job by a surgeon. And the frigging press blew it out of proportion. You know, if the woman had done it he would have rewarded her. If she didn't want to do it, well and good, he can get it from someone else. End of story. But the so called free press was all over us. We had to show that we have reformed. So the bloody president organizes this sham. And we all had to change our plans to attend this rubbish. I would rather have been at the races in another continent." He paused for a second and then continued his monologue "But everything happens for a reason, they say. Had it not been for this event I would never have had a chance to have the company of a beautiful woman like you, that too when my wife is away at the races! Don't get me wrong. I have known a lot of pretty women in my life but you will beat them all hands down!"

Gamma could feel the blood rushing to her face. Even in the dimly lit surroundings she knew that everyone would notice her blush. And flattery from this powerful man was making her heady. Was she being seduced by him? She would control things and keep everything within decent limits, she thought.

Chapter 16

The chit chat in the after party was quite interesting. But she also knew that another few days with this crowd would destroy her soul.

"Come on girl, have another glass of this port. It is very expensive, you know. I opened this bottle especially for you. I have been around many wineries in many continents but this is the best." The theme echoed the sentiment of the evening: we are one powerful people but you are the best and you are getting the best. It made her feel powerful and strong. And the alcohol was playing tricks on her body. Her feet and hands were tingling. The eyes felt heavy. But she felt more alive than ever before in her life. Did he laze my drink with something, she thought.

"We are the core group that controls everything," one of them said. "You are in the sanctum sanctorum of the Guild. Anything we decide will be the policy of the Guild. From those days the Kings, Clergy and the Shamans have ruled society. Now the Kings are no more. They are replaced by the elected officials who will vanish in a few years. The clergy has been discredited. So at present the doctors are the most trusted segment of society. The upper crust so to speak."

"And we the surgeons are the most visible group of doctors." interjected another of the elite group. "It is because of what we do. Everybody likes an action hero. We are the action men of medicine."

At this point her partner for the outing introduced her to the group as Gamma, a friend. They were not interested in what she did and other such minutiae. "Where did you pick up this pretty woman?" asked some in chorus. Some had come with their wives while others came with "other" women. The wives appeared to tolerate their husbands' rowdy behavior quite well. Many had been nurses and had seen their respective husbands grow in stature and power over the years. For them their behavior was the norm in hospitals. There was nothing wrong.

"Most of us happen to be vascular surgeons at this time. It is not that we planned it this way. But in the musical chairs that we play with positions in the Guild, many vascular surgeons have ended up on the right chairs and so we shall rule for the next few years."

"Don't take him seriously and go away thinking the craft groups are competing with each other for power. At the end of the day we are all friends and we look after each other." This gentleman must not have been a vascular surgeon.

At this time a tall bespectacled gentleman in blazers entered. "Here comes the Rottweiler!" remarked Gamma's partner.

"Why do you call him a dog?" she asked. She was getting drunker with this power talk, more drunk than any liquor could ever make her.

"Ha ha we have a few. This one is Alsatian; then we have bull dogs; we even have Piranhas."

"What do you mean?" she asked.

"How do you think we retain our power? Power these days doesn't flow from guns. Nor does it flow from virtuous living. It flows from gaining the confidence of the society. This confidence thingy is a make believe concept. Not everyone can gain confidence. It is like Microsoft cornering the Windows market. We make people believe that we maintain standards. The politicians are scared to question us. So whatever we say goes in society."

"So people will think he is a Rottweiler if you say so?" asked Gamma.

"No we call him that amongst ourselves only. It is our pet name for him. We love him. He serves an important function."

"I don't get you."

"You see, every surgeon gets complications. It is inevitable. Unlike people who don't do procedures, we are vulnerable. Our outcomes can be measured. And invariably there will be complaints. The complaints are a big headache to the administrators and the politicians. They had to address them to maintain credibility. Here's where we come in. We say "outsource" the complaints to us. I mean not every single complaint but those that they have to deal with properly. Once we get the complaints we assign them to one of our "medical experts." If we want the complaints to be killed we have a few softies, you may call them Golden Retrievers or Yorkies. On the other hand if we want to get an adverse finding we have our team of Rottweilers and Piranhas. They will find fault even if the surgeon coughs during the operation. They are good at fine combing the medical records and highlighting the uncrossed 't' s and undotted 'i' s. And we achieve what we want. Do you understand now?"

Suddenly it dawned on Gamma that these guys were smarter than the politicians, smarter than the media and they were indeed ruling the roost. On the one hand it scared the hell out of her but on the other she felt very special to have caught the attention of these power brokers. She thought of Lambda. Poor soul, god bless him. He had no chance against this Mafia.

"So what type are you?" she asked.

"I am a gold fish with teeth..." he smiled. He elaborated. I hold many positions. I am popular. I cannot afford to look like a bully or a Rottweiler. So I am nice to people. And I most often do help people. I have quashed many complaints. So the surgeons love me. But there are few who have managed to rub me on the wrong side. Then I have killed their careers without them even realizing they were being destroyed, all the time believing that I was trying to help."

"What is the difference between a Rottweiler and a Piranha?" she was bemused with the terminology.

"Piranhas do the job slowly." He was proud of the names he had selected.

The jive talk was all getting too much for her. She was slowly beginning to think like them; and act like them.

She felt overwhelmed by the power that was thick in the air in the room. The group had their own private corner in the bar. They met here whenever there was a function or a conference in the city. The after party was where many strategic decisions were taken. It was a place for the power brokers to chew the cud and for the junior inductees to form lasting bonds.

"Now we can let go of the pretentions. Let us just be ourselves," said one loosening his bow tie. Ties came off and sleeves got rolled up. Shirts were unbuttoned half way just as the coats found their ways to the backs of the chairs. The waitresses too had suddenly turned into young buxom ladies. Gone were the men in tight shirts and the middle aged women. The music turned into romantic slow numbers. Some couples were dancing. The banter turned more rowdy.

There were lots of double meaning jokes and sexual innuendos. The surgeons seemed to thrive in putting people down. Even amidst the groups the talk was more one-upmanship and undermining others. No one seemed to mind. They gave as good as they got.

"My Merc is too old," said one. It has been two years since I got a new car."

"I can sell you my Ferrari," said another. "The question is whether you can afford it."

"I know how you bought the Ferrari! You spent half your life looking up people's bums!"

"That's why we tell you vascular surgery is the best," said Gamma's partner for the night.

"Yeah yeah. If you stack the number of prosthetic legs in your city it will reach the moon!" said another.

"Mars is the new moon. Try to reach Mars, and you can make us feel jealous!" said the man with the Ferrari.

"We know that rotten legs paid for the tiles on your swimming pool," said another. They were ganging up against the vascular surgeons.

"I object to these insinuations. We have the audit to prove that we are doing a fine job," the vascular surgeon stood his ground, throwing up his hand in mock helplessness. "They ask for an audit. We are the first to take up the challenge. They still talk about amputation rates!"

"Your fucking audit! How can you rely on an audit that is self reported and confidential? If you look at the survival from ruptured aneurysms you will think you are in wonderland!" said another.

"Yeah any self reported audit is likely to involve gaming. Many patients with slight belly ache and an innocent aneurysm would be classed as ruptured aneurysm!"

"Hey don't get carried away! If we don't enter the data ourselves who will enter it for us? How can we rely on data entered by third parties?" The vascular surgeon was on the defensive.

"That's why I say these are wasteful exercises. I don't think it will stack up in a court of law!"

"Sh! Gentlemen! You don't seem to understand the purpose of these mechanisms. Audits and such review activities are there to show the public that we are transparent and we act in a responsible manner with self monitoring. It is up to the individual to use them in whatever way they want to use them. For example you have an idea of how you are doing. But you shouldn't compare with others. That is a gimmick for the public. So if you enter only true ruptured aneurysms in your data you will get your true results. Rubbish in, rubbish out!"

The man next to Gamma had the last word on these matters.

"You guys seem to be at each other's throats all the time," said Gamma.

"Oh this is how high society works. This is the only place where we can relax and give vent to our feelings. At all other times we are pretending, trying to be politically correct. But we are brothers in arms. We will get together as soon as someone attacks us. So don't worry, we are very good friends"reassured Gamma's partner.

It was true. This was a new experience for her. They all trusted each other and were able to trash one another in jest. The women, many of them long suffering wives, were used to it. WAGs, in the sense of sportsmen. The new ones were in awe as these powerful men tried to outsmart each other in light hearted conversation.

"I can see the brotherhood and camaraderie prevailing here. I can imagine what will happen if the surgeons start to gang up on an outsider. You guys are fucking smart!" She said it! She couldn't believe that she just said the 'F' word. She was not one who used that kind of language with outsiders. She had just met all of these persons. Yet she seemed to be losing her inhibitions. Was it the alcohol or the power that was making her drunk? Was it all the testosterone swirling in the room? But she knew she was changing, and changing fast.

"We are not only fucking smart, we are smart fuckers too," said her suitor, not wanting to lose this opportunity to introduce the sexual slang into their lexicon. "You see that guy in the right corner, he is with his third girl in four years. I am counting the official girlfriends only."

Somehow that made her feel uncomfortable. Women were being objectified and degraded. But there was an allure to this group. They had the power. And they knew how to use it.

"Now that you are an insider, let me tell you. We are enjoying unprecedented power at present. I don't know how long it will last. But even the Commerce Commission, though it has looked into us, is unable to do anything against us. We select the trainees. We select the ones whom we think will fit in. That many of them happen to be sons and daughters is just a coincidence'" he winked as he continued. "Then we train them. If any of them don't conform, we chuck them out. By this we maintain a close knit family. Whenever someone rebels, we have our ways to put them in place. This is where Rottweilers and Piranhas are useful. Even the ministers ask for our advice when appointing members for the regulatory boards. So we have full control. Especially in smaller specialties like vascular and plastics; everyone knows everyone else. The bad apples would have been cast away on the way, so we end up with only the really nice people. If someone wants to live with us according to our rules, they will be fine. If they get other ideas, heavens will strike them down." Saying this he smiled again. He was holding her hand in his, and gently massaging the back of her hand with his other hand. Somehow it was soothing. She felt very safe and secure in his care.

"What about doctors who train overseas and join in the middle?" she asked. "Mm! Those unfortunate souls. They should have stayed in their countries. If they come here, they have to play by our rules. They have to join our training. Whatever they did in their past lives doesn't count. They may have done a thousand aneurysms elsewhere. But it counts for zilch! Zero! When they come here they are born again. Many of them end up becoming family physicians or internists. This way we keep it within the family."

He continued "But we need some overseas trained guys to hold the fort while the anointed ones finish training. We call them fill-in-the-gap people, or seat warmers. They help to keep our on-call rosters from becoming too onerous. As soon as the heir apparent comes they need to make way. If they stay and fight we will unleash the wrath of the surgical gods on them."

"So you create all these obstacles to minimize competition?" asked Gamma. By now his hands were massaging her elbow. She felt attracted to him like he was a magnet. She felt weak and limp. She could not resist. His boasts of authority over the lives of others seemed to have the same effect on her. She was under his control.

"The real money is in private practice. But we need public hospitals where we can treat complex patients and those who cannot go private. And we treat the public patients only to keep the primary doctors happy. When they ring us they know that we will treat the patient in one place or another. But the suckers from overseas, by the time they come through all the hoops they would have lost the best years of their careers. Many of them will settle in small towns and remote places. If anyone manages to come near the main cities it will be when they are quite old. With all these hardships they would have lost their drive to establish and expand. "

"You seem to have everything in place for self preservation," said Gamma, with a hint of admiration in her voice. His hands had reached her upper arm by this time.

"Have you heard of the second hit theory?" asked the amorous surgeon with a chuckle. He was well advanced in his conquest. He was on a roll with his bravado. Here was an admirer willing to listen with starry eyes.

"Second hit is a common phenomenon which we see in body's immune responses. My second hit is when we destroy a surgeon. You see, when we target someone, we precipitate complaints and reviews. Most careers will buckle under this pressure. It will take years for them to clear their names, if at all. They will be like hamsters on a wheel. Most will give up. The process will sap any fight left in them. But there are some motherfuckers who are very resilient. They somehow fight their way through everything we throw at them. That is when we implement the second hit. With their credibility already threadbare, they will just be obliterated by a second wave of complaints."

He hugged her tightly as he leaned into her face, the lips almost touching. "Have you heard of the two Christchurch earthquakes? The first one was much stronger but most buildings withstood it quite well; and there were no deaths. The second tremor, a few months later, was much smaller but a lot of buildings, that had been structurally weakened in the first quake, collapsed, leading to a lot of destruction and loss of life. That is what we mean by second hit, to a surgeon's career."

She was in his power; under his control. Her eyes were half closed as their lips met. His one hand was on her breasts and his other on her thigh, trying to find a way through the barriers of clothing. The others seemed to be oblivious to this romantic interlude. Perhaps they were busy in their own private moments.

She was on the verge of surrender. Another conquest for him. She wanted to keep the conversation going. She was indeed drunk in his power; his absolute power over the lives of many. He looked like Adonis in her eyes, at that moment.

"So where does the patient fit in, in all of this scheme of things?" she asked, more out of a necessity to talk something, than in any inquisitiveness or enquiry.

"Ah! Good thing you asked. The patients are just a nuisance in all this power play. They are a necessary inconvenience. You see, most complaints originate from staff, not patients!" He looked at her with callous disregard. "The patients are just pawns in our games of chess. Nothing more; nothing less."

It was like she had been hit by a thousand bolts of lightening. She woke up from her state of intoxication with a start! What was she doing with this man? Why was she allowing him to take liberties with her. She did not belong to this group. She was like Ruth amid the alien corn. This was not where she wanted to be. Doctors existed for the patients. The patients were the only reason the doctors came into being. Had there been no patients, there would have been no doctors. What was this man talking about and what was she doing allowing herself to be seduced by this vile man? Memories of the sexual harassment she endured at the television company came flooding back. And the innocent face of Lambda was smiling at her, mocking her for this indiscretion.

"Stop it!" she screamed. She pushed him away.

"Hey girl stop putting up fake resistance. All you bitches are the same. You want money and status. You try to raise the stakes by putting up this kind of bullshit! I will have you squirming in my bed very soon, bitch!" He tried to kiss her forcibly. His face hovered over hers menacingly.

But she was strong. She pushed him away with all her might. "Thud!" with a loud noise she slapped him and got away from him.

"Please don't create a scene. My reputation will be gone. I beg you!" He was now pleading with her. All the confidence that he showed minutes earlier had evaporated suddenly. He was shaking. He was a defeated man.

"Today was the day when you proudly proclaimed that you are going to treat women with respect! What a fucking hypocrite!" She thundered as she got up.

"Oh please. I beg you. I will do anything you want me to do. Please let's keep this private."

"Kiss my ass!" she said. "I will do anything, please forgive and forget this episode. I plead with you. Once again I tell you. I will do anything you want me to do!"

"Anything?" she asked. She was actually smiling now. A mysterious smile. She had regained her composure. She was fully in control of herself.

"So, Mr. Creepy Hypocrite, you will do anything I ask you to do if I do not report this sexual harassment incident? You can do with some respect for starters. Why don't you call me madam, from now onwards?"

"Yes madam. Let's keep this private. I promise you; I will do anything that you ask me to do."

Chapter 17

Mr. Theta was pacing up and down his office, lost in deep thought. Lambda was slouched in the chair in front of his large leather top mahogany table. His shoulders slumped and his hands on his chin. He looked a defeated man.

"I have looked everywhere in the country. No one is willing to give an expert opinion," said the lawyer, in a worried tone.

"Am I a hopeless case then? Are my actions so indefensible?" asked Lambda.

"Not that at all. I wouldn't have taken up your case if it was hopelessly lost before we began. So that is not the issue. Nobody is willing to go in public to testify against Alpha. He is the president of the Vascular Federation."

"They are not testifying against Alpha. They are just giving their opinion in a case where he has made allegations."

"You and I may see it that way. But the world doesn't see it like that at all. The vascular world especially. It is Alpha versus you. And it is not just about giving a written opinion. It is about standing up in a court and defending that opinion. Anyone who does that will cross Alpha's path. You know how vengeful he is. People are just scared of him. People are scared to antagonize him lest his anger turns against them."

"Yes Beta called him a psychopath."

"That was then, my dear Lambda. But now Beta is firmly in his camp. Why the hell did you come in his sights? You should have avoided him like a plague."

"But he would have had to get rid of either Beta or me. I had no chance!"

"No! Had you not started your own vascular lab, and played your cards well, it would have been Alpha and you versus Beta."

"I could not have forgiven myself if I had compromised on my principles and got involved in an intrigue to get rid of another surgeon."

"You and your principles. I have to tell you you are bloody naive. Anyway you are in this situation and we need to deal with it. Let me think more about whom we approach." Mr. Theta really liked this man, though he was annoyed by his lack of street smartness.

"In know I did not do anything wrong. Why can't I testify on my own behalf!"

""Your word doesn't count. It is your expert versus his. Whoever has the bigger clout will win. It doesn't matter who tells the truth. It doesn't matter what the outcome was. It only matters what the expert thinks was the right thing to do, in that patient at that time. So you need a heavyweight in the field who is willing to support your actions strongly. Half hearted attempts won't do. It would be wiser to plead guilty and show that you have insight into your failings, rather than try to defend yourself using a weak expert or no expert at all."

"That will be justice done?"

"My friend, law is an ass. We have to play the game in their terrain with their rules. Truth doesn't matter. It is about giving the appearance that truth is on your side. That's all."

"So why can't we find an expert?" asked Lambda, still puzzled.

"Because this is Alpha's domain." said Theta.

"Can't we go outside his sphere of influence, can't we go overseas to look for an expert?" asked Lambda.

"Eureka!" shouted Mr. Theta. "You said it! In fact I have already made some enquiries. The logistics will be difficult! In my long years of practice never have I had to secure a foreign expert. But in your case that is our only option!"

That settled, they discussed other strategy. "You help me draft response to clinical issues. Also please look at this document which lists the distortions, abuse, vilification, put downs and ganging ups in the complaint document lodged by Alpha. It is a shocking disgrace. He had no business to use derogatory and abusive terminology even if he had concerns about your practice. There is a code of conduct that binds medical practitioners, when dealing with other practitioners. His breaches go beyond human decency. We need to bring this to the notice of the authorities even though I doubt if they will take any action against him. It is an unfair world."

Pausing for a few seconds he added "If he had made these statements in ordinary circumstances you could have sued him out of his pants and completely destroyed him. But he has made it under the guise of making a notification against you. He has used very bad language so much so that any outsider who has no idea about the internal politics and how he brought his son to your position, would think very badly of you, especially coming from a person of high standing such as the president of the Vascular Federation. Unfortunately the law protects him from being sued. It is ironic. The protection in the law is to empower the weak and the meek so that they can speak out. But he has used that loophole to destroy you."

"Nevertheless we need to point out his transgressions to the authorities. But what will clinch the matter for you is defeating him on clinical issues, not on his bad conduct.

" The other issue is the legitimacy of the hearing that banned you. If we can prove that Dr Vector had a conflict of interest that he did not declare, the hearing would lose its legitimacy. It would be akin to a mistrial. But the burden of proof is on us, not them. We are working on multiple sources regarding this issue. I am hoping to hit the jackpot soon.

"Also if you have emails that will prove that the head of the department asked you to go for further training and then installed his son in your place it will strengthen your case. Remember you are not going to get any relief for the loss of job in this hearing. But this is your opportunity to place this issue before the public. As you know you have missed all your deadlines for the employment tribunal. You were lulled into a false sense of security by this master manipulator. By placing this issue in front of the press you may move someone to see the blatant injustice done to you, and take some action."

"Our tactics should be multipronged but it is the clinical front that is important. Others are secondary."

"Where is Gamma," asked Lambda.

"Hasn't she been in contact with you? She sends me emails from time to time. But she specifically asked me not to discuss her with you. I think she doesn't want to distract you."

Distract him? She was the only one with whom he could share his mind openly without thinking about the consequences. It was not very often that one feels connected to someone at a deep level. And she had disappeared suddenly from his life. What was she thinking? Has she found another lover? It was very hard for him to swallow the fact that she was talking to his lawyer about his matters but was avoiding him. Why was she playing games?

The more he tried to probe Mr. Theta, the more evasive the legal man became. He advised him to concentrate on his upcoming case, and forget about everything else. This only made his longing for her even more than before. He was more worried about losing her than losing his career at that point. But little could he do, to change the situation.

He felt that his head would explode if he did not know what happened to Gamma. He knew she went to the other city to attend a Guild of Surgeons function and then have a vacation. He knew that she had contacted Theta. Why was she avoiding him? Had she abandoned him? Had she hooked up with a surgeon at the Guild who has now turned her against Lambda? It was a dirty world, this world of surgeons. No one could trust anyone else. And just because of their short fling he could not expect her to be on his side forever. He was a loser. The ones whom she would have met at the function were all successful people. Most of them would have been Alpha's friends. Lambda did not own her.

In his self doubt he could not stop imagining the worst. An idle mind is a dangerous thing. He wondered if she was actually sabotaging Theta's work by side tracking him into irrelevant minutiae. A wild goose chase; like the one he was sent on by Alpha.

He chided himself for doubting her integrity. If she was sleeping with the enemy she would have told him up front. She was a very honorable person. Why would she try to harm him? He was certainly beginning to have feelings for her. Was he becoming too possessive? The more he tried to get rid of her thoughts the more he thought about her. His mind was like the meditative mind of a novice trying to cut out all thoughts, only to end up thinking about the thoughts.

And the D-Day was coming up very fast. He felt an excitement and anticipation. But he also felt an apprehension and fear. If the judges were neutral they would surely see his point of view, and exonerate him in the least. If he was lucky they may criticize the conduct of Alpha and the hospital. But what if they were biased? His interactions with the system had not inspired confidence in their neutrality. Some days he would wake up with a sweat having dreamed that they had upheld the ban, and banned him for life. Who was to question them if they decided to do that. Accountability was not a word that was in their dictionary. The draconian system was loaded against the accused doctor.

Like this the days went by quickly and his tryst with the court came soon enough. Still no sign of Gamma, though he learned from Theta that she had sent some material for his examination.

Chapter 18

The courtroom was intimidating. It was very formal and impersonal. To make it worse there was a press gallery. The press loves the stories about rogue doctors. Every national and regional paper was represented. The preliminaries were taken care of by both parties in a methodical exchange of papers. In fact there had been a dispositions hearing where most procedures had been agreed upon.

On one side were the lawyers from the Medical Board, and their medical expert, one of the well known Rottweilers in the Guild of Surgeons. On the other side, flanking Lambda was the legal team led by Mr. Theta on the right and the medical experts from overseas on the left. Yes there were two, not one, overseas medical experts. Though Theta had told him who the experts were, the sight of them was awe inspiring. One was a well known vascular surgery professor who was considered an authority in many areas of vascular surgery. The other was an equally famous radiologist who had pioneered the very procedure that Lambda was accused of performing inappropriately in one of the charges.

Lambda had seen the international experts at the major conferences. They were the go to people in their respective fields. Their body language and mannerisms showed that they were on top of their game and commanded mastery over their subjects. And it was very obvious that they were respected by all and sundry in the field.

It gave him hope. Hope where there had been none before. There had been setback after setback lately. Now things may be turning around. He may have some respite. The relentless attack by Alpha on his whole persona may be stopped now.

They took up the first case. The expert for the Board seemed to be very happy that this case was taken up first. He said "I am in the reserve army and I have a lot of experience in training younger surgeons in dealing with military trauma. We run a course on how to open the chest in acute situations. We recommend that the chest be opened through the middle, through the breast bone. So what this doctor did was wrong. It was below the standard expected of a surgeon of similar training'" he thundered. The panel members were nodding in agreement. Oops! He had opened the account with a home run. It would be difficult to recover from this, thought Lambda. He was doomed.

Now it was the turn of the vascular surgery professor. "Tell me doctor," he asked his rival, looking through the upper part of his glasses, a professorial look indeed. He paused for maximum effect. "How many civilian trauma cases have you done where you have had to open the chest, in the past ten years? I have done none!"

The air was pregnant with expectation as everyone awaited the military man's answer.

Answer came after a few seconds. The thunder in his voice had disappeared. "None," he muttered feebly.

"In military trauma the high velocity bullets and shrapnel will cause damage to all parts of the chest. Therefore opening the chest in the middle is the best strategy to enable access to all corners of the chest cavity. But this was a solitary stab injury. And you know exactly where the wound is. In my opinion going across the chest gives the quickest entry into the chest." Saying this he paused again, looking deep into the other doctor's eyes. "How many emergency room thoracotomies have you done in the last 10 years?"

Another feeble reply came, after some hesitation confirming that this doctor had not done any emergency thoracotomies in 10 years.

He turned towards the panel and proclaimed expansively "Gentlemen, emergency room thoracotomy is done when there is a definitive evidence of where the injury is, and the patient is dying, like this patient was. But the outcomes are appalling. Most patients would die in spite of this procedure."

He turned towards Lambda. "Doctor, what happened to your patient?" he asked. He was reveling in the courtroom experience. He could have become a great actor if he had wanted to.

"He walked home in 10 days, sir!"

"Did he have any disability?"

"None sir, except for mild pain in the scar."

Mr. Theta turned towards the judges. "A patient who should have died goes home in perfect health in ten days. But the doctor who saved his life is being persecuted several years down the track. This is a disgrace!"

That seemed to have sorted the first case. Lambda one. Alpha love. But there was a lot to get through. The second case came up quickly.

This was a case of ruptured aortic aneurysm where the patient had been found at home in extremis, and had a cardiac arrest soon after the operation commenced. The patient was revived; Lambda clamped the aorta but needed help from Beta to complete the operation. After Beta left, Lambda noticed that the right leg had no palpable pulse. Therefore he wanted to do an embolectomy, which involved exposing the femoral artery in the groin and passing a balloon catheter to remove any clots in the leg. The operating room staff insisted that he had to wait for staff changeover. The patient was under anesthesia. The patient was kept warm in the operating room and was being monitored. Even if the patient had been sent to the intensive care unit the patient would have been left under anesthesia at least for twenty four hours on artificial breathing as was usual in such cases. So there was no point fighting with the dysfunctional nursing unit. Lambda had waited and did the embolectomy after the staff changeover.

The outcome: the patient went home in 2 weeks! Again this was a patient who had more than eighty percent chance of dying. And Lambda was facing charges after a prolonged 'investigation.'

The charges: That he did not clamp the aorta within few minutes of the operation. This was a fabrication. Lambda could clearly remember having to deal with adhesions in the upper abdomen before he could clamp the aorta. He first had his fingers across the artery and then, having cleared the way to be able to see the aorta, he applied the clamp on the aorta. He could clearly remember calling out the time which should have been entered in the patient records by the nurses. Whether it was due to the general dysfunctional nature of the environment or whether there was a deliberate attempt to frame him, the time was not recorded.

Yet from the fact that the patient survived the operation and left the hospital in two weeks it could be surmised that the clamp was applied expeditiously, thereby preventing the patient from suffering consequences of uncontrolled bleeding.

The accusation just fell off when the expert opined that his client had saved a patient who had a very high chance of death. But the allegation that he waited for the change of staff instead of pushing on made for interesting argument.

The fact was that the operating room was very dysfunctional. Some nursing staff were unruly. The management tolerated this. Alpha, the head of the department, had actively undermined Lambda. So insisting that they do the operation before staff changeover would have led to a lot of recriminations.

"So doctor, what would have been different had the embolectomy been done immediately?" asked Mr. Theta, of the Medical Board expert.

"The patient would have been returned to the intensive care unit earlier," said the expert, unable to figure out what was coming.

"And?" asked Mr. Theta, with the question hanging in the air.

"He would have been managed in the intensive care unit," he said, puzzled.

"We all know that doctor. But what would they have done differently?" asked Mr. Theta. Turning towards Lambda's expert he asked "Can you answer?"

"Not much. They would have left the patient on artificial ventilation for at least 24 hours, which means the patient would have continued to be under general anesthesia. They would have kept the patient warm and monitored the vital parameters, which was already being done in the operating room. They would have done baseline blood tests which were done in the operating room too."

"Would going to the ICU earlier have made any difference?" asked Mr. Theta, still looking at his own expert.

"You mean the patient who should have died, but went home in 14 days, would have left one day earlier?" the expert said, in a voice hardly concealing his amusement.

"I think we can move to the next case," said the chairman, coming to the rescue. The expert may have lived to fight another case but his score was rapidly turning bad. Lambda two; Alpha love.

The next case was where Dr Lambda was accused of doing an aortic bypass and a femoral popliteal bypass in one sitting. "This is dangerous! It should not have been done together!" The medical expert's voice was somewhat muted compared to his original tone. After the first two bruising encounters he had lost his momentum. On the other hand Lambda's expert was on the ascendancy. His demeanor was becoming progressively more dominant.

"Multilevel bypass is perfectly acceptable. We do it all the time. In fact we recently set a question about this in the recertification exam. The answer is that multilevel bypass is the preferred option in these circumstances. If that was the patient's preference, that is what should be offered." His voice thundered over that of his rival. Turning to the judges he said "This patient went home in ten days, had no untoward side effects and still has the leg, which was saved by Lambda's intervention."

"But," countered the other expert. "He used a transverse incision going across the abdomen. He should have used a vertical incision. Also he should have reversed the vein after harvesting it for the bypass."

"Let me explain to you my dear judges: the aorta can be approached from vertical transverse or retroperitoneal approaches, the last one approaching the artery from the left side. All are acceptable. Clinical trials done comparing these incisions have not shown any difference whatsoever. The approach used is entirely surgeon's preference. None of these are better or worse than the other. Similarly when the leg vein is used to bypass a blocked artery, the problem of valves has to be addressed. The veins contain valves and the direction of blood flow is opposite to that of the arteries. The valve problem can be overcome by either cutting the valves or changing the orientation of the vein by reversing it upside down. If the valves are cut, the vein can be left in the same anatomical location it was, which is called in situ bypass, or the vein can be placed in a deeper tunnel, which is called translocated bypass. All of these techniques are correct."

He looked at his opposite number in a derisive way. "If you have done enough number of operations you would be familiar with all of these techniques."

Mr. Theta did not want to miss the opportunity. He ambushed the Medical Board expert. "How many aortic and femoral popliteal bypasses have you done doctor?"

"I cannot tell you off hand."

"But you participate in the national audit, don't you doctor? So this information should be just a few clicks away on your laptop." Theta had nailed it.

"The audit is privileged information. I cannot divulge that." The expert protested.

"Yes you can! You can voluntarily submit your numbers. It will only solidify your standing as an expert, if you show us that you have done thousands of these operations."

Was he sarcastic or was he genuine? He was smiling.

One of the judges picked up the cue. "Let us note that the medical expert will provide his numbers from the audit tomorrow. Let us move to the next case."

The next one was about a patient who had a ruptured iliac artery during a procedure. Dr Lambda had immediately passed a guide wire and a balloon over it. The inflated balloon straddled the area and temporarily plugged the hole. He then wanted to deploy a covered stent which would have sealed the breach. Ordinary stents are made of metal mesh, providing a scaffolding to keep an artery open. Covered stents have a covering of fabric in addition, which provides a water tight seal in the area where the covered stent is deployed.

Unfortunately there was no covered stent available in the hospital. Unfazed, Lambda called other hospitals in the region and also the company. Finally a stent was couriered from the company warehouse in Big Smoke. In spite of the delay the patient was stable throughout.

"You should have opened up the belly and sutured the hole." The opposite expert was seeking to regain lost ground.

"No!" intervened the internationally renown radiologist, testifying on behalf of Lambda. "Vascular surgery is a rapidly changing field and Dr Lambda's method of control of bleeding was perfectly acceptable, and in fact, it is the preferable way of dealing with these sudden emergencies!"

The more he delved into the technical details the more his lack of expertise was exposed. Even the judges could sense that the Medical Board's expert witness was a dinosaur in his field. Again he had come up short against Lambda's experts.

The next allegation was about handover of a patient who had a threatened leg due to lack of blood flow. Lambda had had to leave in a hurry due to a family emergency. The allegation was that he failed to handover the patient to another surgeon.

Well, how well could one handover patients? Face to face is nearly impossible when two busy surgeons had to handover to each other. But Mr. Theta had the trump card. He produced the telephone log which showed that Lambda had called Dr Beta twice prior to leaving. The first one was on the previous night and the next on the morning of his departure, just before boarding the plane.

"He had spoken for five minutes and two minutes respectively. Do you think they were discussing the weather?" Then he delivered the coup de grace: an email correspondence between Lambda and a junior resident which implied that Beta had accepted the handover and was going to see the patient.

"If you are not convinced, let me show you a copy of the patient's medical records. There were two entries there saying Beta had seen the patient. If he saw the patient he did nothing. The patient was left with an ischemic leg that Lambda had to remove on his return in a few days time.

"If this is not proof that a hand over had taken place, what is proof? The fact is that Dr Beta did nothing. If you are prosecuting Lambda for not handing over you are barking at the wrong tree. If Dr Beta had seen this patient he is guilty of not acting promptly. But there is a bigger problem here."

Pausing for effect he delivered the check mate. "There are two copies of the medical records, made during the different reviews that Lambda was subjected to. One of them contains Dr Beta's entries. The other doesn't. How can that be, unless Beta had surreptitiously inserted the entries after the first copy had been made. I contend that he feared he would be blamed for not seeing this patient. So he made these entries not knowing that a copy had already been made."

"I object your honor! These could be due to the error of the clerk making the copy. They may have missed a page." The Board's lawyer was on the defensive.

"Look here sir! It is the same page. One has the entry and the other doesn't. The same applies to the second instance too!"

"Altering medical records is a serious criminal offence. We need to look at Dr Beta's conduct in a separate inquiry." The chairperson instructed the Medical Board to investigate this matter and report back to the court within one month.

There was a hushed silence in the courtroom. The journalists who turned up to witness the ritual humiliation of Lambda were seeing a totally different development. The Medical Board was on the defensive. Yet for the journalists it didn't matter who won. This was a battle royal in the court room. Once they knew that Lambda was a victim and not the villain, they started to support Lambda. It would make a huge newsworthy event when the underdog turns tables on the powerful and the mighty.

The expert was intent on somehow making something stick on Lambda. "There won't be smoke without fire!" he said, as he went to the last case for the day. This was the case that led to the suspension of the license. The medical expert believed he had a watertight case.

It was a patient with mixed arterial and venous disease who had recurrent infections and massive swelling of the leg. After treating the veins, Lambda had proceeded to attempt minimally invasive treatment of the arterial blockage. Unfortunately the patient developed an infection in the blocked artery. This was extremely rare. Infection, if any, usually occurred in the artery that is punctured with a needle to gain access into the arterial system.

This was the case where Alpha had made a damning and exaggerated complaint, completely undermining the standing of Lambda as a surgeon. This was the complaint that led to the drastic action on Lambda's license.

"There was no indication for the arterial operation!" exploded the expert. He had regained the thunder in his voice realizing that this was his best chance. "There was smoke. Now we have fire!"

Lambda's expert calmly said "If you sling a bucket load of mud and hope that something will stick, you are mistaken. Yes there is smoke. It is not just smoke. It is smelly putrid smoke arising from a father's attempt to install his son in another doctor's position," as he tabled correspondence between Alpha and Lambda.

The emails were explosive. They showed how Lambda had been duped into leaving his position to go overseas for "further training" and how Alpha pressurized Lambda to accept his son as the stand in, telling the medical director that his son and Alpha were trying to help Lambda. Then there was an email, sent when his son had been ensconced well and truly in Lambda's position where he had asked the medical director not to take Lambda back when he finished his "further training."

"These are distractions. We need to concentrate on the clinical cases." The lawyer to the Medical Board did not want to get drawn into what the complainant, Alpha, had done. He wanted Lambda to be judged in isolation, irrespective of the circumstances.

"I understand Dr Alpha is giving evidence tomorrow. Let us bring this matter up at that time." The chairman wanted to hear the clinical case now. The other matters could all be addressed together the following day.

"This patient did not need an arterial operation! Dr Lambda did an operation without a need." The medical expert was emphatic.

"Well we beg to disagree. The patient had mixed arterial and venous disease. The patient was on the threshold of having an ulcer. It only needed a scratch to start off an ulcer. He had massive swelling of his leg. Besides, there was a history of recurrent infections. The circulation is a continuum. The blood comes through the arteries. And after the exchange of nutrients and oxygen at the capillary bed it goes back to the heart via the veins. This patient had severe arterial and venous insufficiency. If both were not treated and the patient put on compression stockings he would have continued to have problems." Lambda's expert was an international authority. He could not conceal his disdain of his opposite number. The more confident the expert is, the more likely he would carry the day with him. With his international reputation and eloquent display of mastery of the subject, Lambda's expert was steamrolling the Board expert.

Moving to the next point on the same patient the prosecuting expert said "This patient had an abdominal aortic aneurysm. This was not picked up before the operation that Dr Lambda did. Why wasn't an ultrasound of the abdomen not done?"

He had been waiting for this. He pounced on the board's expert. "The patient had no symptoms nor signs of any problems in his aorta. In this country, as far as I understand, there is no funding for screening ultrasounds. Doing an ultrasound when there is no indication for doing one, when Dr Lambda owns the vascular ultrasound facility, would be Medicare fraud!"

It was quite a powerful message; not the least due to the dramatic and articulate delivery. And it was working. The panel were nodding their heads. This man had them eating from his hands. It was like watching a powerful drama.

"And he did an endovascular procedure going from the other side, crossing over. That is fraught with complications."

The accusations were coming thick and fast, even as they were being defended. But this one was a bit silly, thought Lambda. And his expert did not take much time to expose the weakness of his opponent. "You haven't done many of these procedures, have you?" he asked the Rottweiler. "If you had, you will know that the standard approach for treating a flush occlusion of the femoral artery is to go from the other side. If you are suggesting that Dr Lambda should have gone from the same side, you must be either a wizard, like my friend here," he said pointing to the internationally known radiologist in his team. "Or," he continued "you must have very little experience in these procedures." He paused for a moment before delivering the punch line: "I suspect it is the latter."

The whole court was in stunned silence. Never before had they seen a so called medical expert being beaten so badly. This was a new experience for Rottweiler. Until that time he had done the bidding of his friends, and was waterproof under the cloak of the Guild of Surgeons. Even if there were opposite experts who disagreed, there was an unwritten code that they did not humiliate each other in front of others. They were members of the same fraternity. But not this time. Lambda's expert had no qualms about exposing his weaknesses for the entire world to see. The bully had become the bullied.

Trying to recover, the Board expert requested a time out. It was a strategic move. Momentum was building up against him rapidly. He wanted to break his enemy's rhythm.

After the adjournment, when the court reconvened, he seemed to have regained his composure. He said "The patient came to see Dr Lambda few days after the procedure. The patient had leg pain and was sweating. Lambda missed an infection of the artery!" This was a damning allegation. He was sure Lambda could not get out of this.

Mr. Theta tabled a document. It was the weather report for Little Smoke for the day in question, and the days prior to it and after it.

"Looking at this report, where the temperature was unseasonably high and where the humidity was near hundred percent, can you imagine anyone who did not sweat? My client doesn't recall this patient sweating any more or any less than the others. Besides, the patient told him that the pain was improving on paracetamol. The patient did not have any abnormal physical findings. So how could you accuse my client of missing an infection of the artery?"

The international radiologist jumped in. "Infection of the artery, anywhere other than at the site of entry, or the puncture site, is extremely rare. The signs are subtle. And after many nonspecific findings, it suddenly flares up!" He tabled a paper where a similar case had been discussed. "These are extremely rare. I will not find fault with anyone for not spotting the infection at that early stage."

"I put it to you that you falsified records to underplay his illness!" said the Medical Board's expert staring into Lambda's eyes. If only he could discredit this man's integrity, his credibility would be gone, must have been his logic.

"I object to this unsubstantiated allegation!" Mr. Theta intervened on behalf of his client. "On what basis do you throw this allegation?"

"Dr Alpha, president of the Federation, and a senior surgeon, would not have said you falsified records without a reason!"

"Well we will deal with Dr Alpha's integrity and falsification tomorrow. But I want to table this at this juncture." Mr. Theta connected his laptop to the internet and asked Lambda to log into his email. There, in the sent folder, attached to one of the emails were the voice clips of all the patients on whom he dictated letters, in sequence, for that day. "These were sent from his office to the transcription service on the same day. In fact even his Dictaphone with all the sound clips for this day is still available for inspection. You will note, your Honors, that the letters were all typed in exactly the same way as they were dictated, in the same order as he saw the patients. Nothing has been altered. And Dr Lambda had no reason to believe that this patient would come back to haunt him, at that time. So there was no attempt to cover up anything, at anytime." He then tabled the hand written notes, again scanned into Lambda's computer on the same day, which reflected the same.

"This vilification and exaggeration has been the hallmark of Dr Alpha's complaint. We have carefully documented the numerous instances where these are found, in his complaint document." He submitted another document.

"We have summoned Dr Alpha to give evidence tomorrow. We will question him in detail about his conduct tomorrow. Now let us get back to this patient. Do you want to persist with this case still?" He looked at the lawyer from the Board derisively.

"We have a couple more allegations," said the lawyer. His voice was like it was coming from a deep well. It was feeble and Lambda could detect a hint of a tremor.

"The patient got admitted to the small hospital, at No Smoke. Dr Lambda abrogated the patient!"

"Not true again! Dr Lambda did not have admitting rights to this hospital any longer because Dr Alpha usurped him with his son. But the son lives in Big Smoke. That particular week Dr Beta was away on holiday. Dr Alpha does not go to No Smoke. Since Dr Alpha's son lives in Big Smoke, there is no vascular cover for No Smoke on the weeks that Dr Beta is away. This is a major down grading of services, solely because Dr Alpha, the head of the department, replaced Dr Lambda with his own son, as the son does not live in the area. Why can't we see the elephant in the room? Had Lambda had admitting or visiting rights he would have taken care of this patient at No Smoke."

He tabled the vascular roster from No Smoke for that month. There were large gaps in the cover.

"Then he should have taken the patient to the private hospital," shot the prosecuting lawyer. "He operated on this patient!"

"No! The patient was at the emergency department of No Smoke. Dr Lambda was available to give telephone advice and information as requested. But he made it clear that he was not looking after this patient. The patient was under the emergency physicians. Had they wanted Lambda to take over the care of the patient they should have requested him specifically. But they were entertaining other diagnoses, including gastroenteritis, because the patient had diarrhea. The onus was on the emergency physician to arrange for appropriate care. Also the private hospital is twenty miles away. How could you expect my client to take a patient to a far away hospital, without knowing what the diagnosis was."

He then tabled the results of the inquiry into the incident report that Dr Alpha had filed against the emergency physicians for calling Dr Lambda, a doctor with no privileges in No Smoke. "Honorable judges, this inquiry concluded that the emergency physicians were at fault and also highlighted the lack of vascular cover for No Smoke that week. It is indeed a telling report. It highlights what this man has done in his greed to bring his son into Dr Lambda's shoes. He was trying to have the cake and eat it too. His son was, and is still, living in Big Smoke. This is a disgrace!"

Mr. Theta seemed to have the judges' ears. They were nodding in unison.

"When things flared up late evening on day two, Lambda should have called Dr Alpha and handed over this patient."

This was the final attempt of the prosecutor to pin down Lambda.

"When the infection was finally recognized by the emergency doctors, it was due to a sudden deterioration. The doctors called Lambda and suggested that the patient had necrotizing fasciitis, and asked him what to do. There was a series of phone calls culminating in a call from Dr Alpha's resident. No matter who initiated the calls the parting message from the resident was that Dr Alpha would call Lambda if he had any more questions. It was clear that Dr Alpha was going to take care of this patient. And it was ridiculous to expect Lambda to take a patient with suspected necrotizing fasciitis to the private hospital, in the middle of the night. He would have killed the patient. The private hospitals have very thin staff cover at nights."

He then added "My client did try to contact Dr Alpha by phone and by email the next day, to no avail. After Dr Alpha staged the daylight heist of Lambda's career he has not returned any calls or emails from Dr Lambda. He knows what he did was wrong. But he does not want to admit it."

The prosecutor's objections to dragging the personal issue between Lambda and Alpha were overruled.

The proceedings were adjourned at that point, to be resumed the following morning.

"I thought it went very well for you. But don't relax, Don't let up the intensity. We have some surprises for tomorrow." Theta said his good byes as he took the medical experts to their hotel in his car.

For Lambda, it was a sleepless night.

Chapter 19

Lambda was in the subway, travelling to the second day's hearings in Big Smoke. He had not been sleeping well for the past week or so. The previous night was the worst. He slept for two hours in total, in small increments. He did not want to take sleeping tablets. And he just could not meditate, try as he may. And he had counted 5000 sheep before realizing the futility of the exercise.

He was tired and apprehensive. Everyone else was going to work. He felt like a misfit. He should not be among the working crowd. He had been removed from the workforce. He felt like a fraud.

Just then there was an announcement. "Is there a doctor on this train? If you are a doctor please identify yourself to the staff."

It was a moving train. The next station was several minutes away. It turned out that the patient needing assistance was in the next compartment. By the time Lambda reached the scene a crowd had gathered. A young girl was having continuous seizures. Froth was pouring out of a corner of her mouth. There was a guide dog next to her and a medical tag on her wrist. It was obvious that she was having a grand mal seizure, or epileptic fit. The patient seemed to be unaware of her surroundings.

One bearded man had assumed authority over the scenario. He seemed to be giving instructions. "Give her a metal spoon," he barked. Everybody was scrambling to get a spoon. The patient was turning blue. It was apparent to Lambda that her tongue was falling back and obstructing the airway. If this was not rectified immediately she may die.

"Turn her to a side and hold the jaws up," said Lambda.

"Excuse me. Who are you? Are you a doctor?" the man asked, refusing to give up his pole position.

Am I a doctor? thought Lambda. Who am I? A doctor without license. A doctor without license is worse than a non doctor. If he had not spent most of his adult life learning and practicing medicine he would have learned some other trade or life skill. But he did not. He was a zero. A zilch. He had been rendered impotent.

After training for the better part of his life and sacrificing personal pleasures to achieve the knowledge and expertise of a surgeon, leave alone a doctor, he was now a no body. The Medical Board had told him clearly that under no circumstance should he come into contact with a patient. What should he do now? If he touched the patient or gave instructions, the Medical Board may come down hard on him. On the other hand if he stayed there and let the patient die, it will be on his conscience for ever in his life. He slowly walked away from the scene, back to his own compartment. His tail between his legs; totally defeated.

He could hear the patient gasp, even as the man forcibly put the spoon in her hand. The train was delayed at the next station until the paramedics turned up to whisk the patient away.

He saw someone playing a news channel on his mobile phone. "A patient is suspected to have suffered serious brain damage due to an epileptic seizure she had while travelling in the underground. Unfortunately there was no doctor on board. By the time the medical team arrived she had already passed out and was blue. It is suspected that her brain had been deprived of oxygen due to blockage of her airway."

Well it was indeed a bad omen for his hearing. He was overcome by guilt and shame. What was the point of being a doctor if he could not help a patient in need, in a timely manner. He cursed himself. He did not deserve to be a doctor. He was useless. Perhaps the Medical Board was right. He should not have a license to practise. He had failed in his duty to help the patient!

If he was down when he arrived at the courts his spirits were lifted when he saw Gamma in the gallery. She waved at him cheerily. She looked radiant in a red dress. He was seeing her after a long time. He had thought she had ditched him from her life. He would not have blamed her if that was the truth. He was a loser. All he could offer her was struggle after struggle and a miserable melancholy. She deserved better.

The day opened with the last of the clinical cases. Lambda was accused of hiding an injury to the vena cava. This allegation was added late in the piece, after the persecution began. What happened was that the resident had avulsed a branch of the vena cava while placing the self retaining retractor. Though the injury was repaired immediately, the patient, at the end of the operation, went into a coagulopathy, which meant there was bleeding everywhere as the blood would not clot. The coagulopathy was corrected after bringing down blood products from Big Smoke. It was too late for the patient. Lambda had wanted a debrief soon after the incident. But none occurred. He had discussed the case at the morbidity mortality meeting and the case notes were reviewed by the center for clinical excellence, which looked into all deaths. At no time did this allegation ever surface, until the Rottweiler got involved. It was based on a note by one of the nurses.

"This was a later insertion!" thundered Mr. Theta. It was not there until Rottweiler reviewed the records. I put it that this was inserted long after the case, to incriminate Dr Lambda."

"No! It was in the records when I reviewed," countered Rottweiler.

"It may have been there at that time but it was not there when the center for clinical excellence reviewed it! I submit that it was added later."

The nurse was summoned next. After the preliminaries Mr. Theta asked her "Do you know that tampering with medical records is a criminal offence?"

"Yes sir!" said the nurse but her face was ashen. It was obvious to those present that she was shaken by the last statement.

"How long have you known Dr Alpha?" fired the legal eagle. "Twenty five years!" shot back the nurse, not knowing what was coming.

"Did you have a fling with him at any time? You scrubbed for him for many years didn't you?"

"Objection your honors! The private lives of these people should not be dragged into the open!"

By this time the nurse was visibly shaken.

"Objection accepted. You may move on." The chief judge was not going to allow the sordid affairs of doctors and nurses to be brought into public domain.

"Ok let's leave that. But did you get a promotion recently? Were you promoted to become the director of the operating room complex over the head of three better qualified candidates?"

"Baseless allegations!" interjected the Board lawyer. But this time the judges did not stop Theta.

"Do you know that falsifying medical records is a criminal offence? You can go to jail and be struck off the nursing register!" Theta knew he was onto something. He wanted to strike while the iron was hot.

"You can confess now and plead for leniency. But if you deny the truth here in a court of law and are then proven to have done it, you will also be convicted of lying in a court of law. We are thinking of minimum five years without parole!"

Theta wanted to drive the nail in her coffin then and there.

"Sentencing is our prerogative. But you should tell the truth at all times!" The judge intervened, stopping Theta from bullying her further.

She was crying by now. "I will tell the truth. Dr Alpha summoned me to his office about a year ago. He had drafted this insertion. He wanted me to write this in my own handwriting and add it to the notes. We have been friends for many years. Besides he was going to be on the interview panel for my promotion. I had no option but to comply!"

There was a shocked silence in the court room. Gamma was smiling. In fact it was her piece of detective work that was paying dividends now. All the hard work by her contacts had unearthed a lot of hidden truths. Even Rottweiler was taken aback by this revelation. Even though he was a friend of Alpha, this one was done without his knowledge. Yes Alpha was a smooth operator. His right hand did not know what his left hand was doing. Even his friends did not know when he was genuine or when he was manipulating them.

Theta did not want to miss this opportunity. "I am appalled by the lackadaisical approach to the sanctity of medical records in this hospital. We just saw one instance of falsifying records. Yesterday we saw how Dr Beta had possibly falsified a patient's chart."

"That instance is not proven." the Board lawyer defended Beta.

"Not yet!" shot Theta. We will get to the bottom of it soon."

The chief judge instructed the Board to initiate a separate inquiry into how the medical records were safeguarded from tampering, at the hospital.

"We take a dim view of the frequency of instances where tampering has occurred. But that inquiry is not related to Dr Lambda's suspension. The purpose of this court is to determine if Dr Lambda is safe to practice." The judge wanted to avoid the distractions and concentrate on the main purpose. But the Board's case had been damaged severely by the lack of credibility of medical records in that hospital.

The next witness was Dr Alpha. The real McCoy! The godfather of vascular surgery in Little Smoke; the president of the Vascular Federation for the whole country; and the man who made the complaint which resulted in Lambda's suspension.

Lambda did not know why Alpha had been summoned. He looked at Alpha for the first time in eighteen months. Yes the friendly figure who had arranged for him to go for "further training"; the man who had offered to help him by lending his own son to look after his practice while he was away. This was the man who had been a hero to him at one time. He would have happily stayed prostrated at his feet, doing his bidding, had he not betrayed him. Why did he kill the harmless mocking bird? His son could have worked in Big Smoke and visited Little Smoke to do some private practice. Lambda would have happily accommodated that. But alas! You cannot turn the clock back. Here was the Macbeth who murdered his career. He was still trying to wash his hands clean. But the blood was not going away!

Lambda looked at Alpha. But the latter avoided eye to eye contact. Was this the same person who charmed Lambda with nostalgic talk about the sport and the heroes that they mutually loved? It appeared that he looked a bit weary and tired. But he still had a commanding demeanor.

After the mundane earthly parts that they had to go through Mr. Theta finally had his chance to interrogate the villain in chief. But he was determined to keep the veneer of calm and respect for as long as possible.

"You are the president of the Vascular Federation and a senior vascular surgeon?"

"Yes I am." said the witness.

We are honored to have you here. Can you elaborate what the functions of the Federation are please? We know you do a great job but we need to hear it for the benefit of the audience here."

"We function as the go-to group in our specialty in this country."

"What does that mean please?" asked Theta.

"We help in training and education. We are responsible for the selection and evaluation of trainees. We maintain standards. We advise the politicians on matters related to our specialty. And we advocate for the vascular surgeons."

"So how do you decide on the number of trainees taken into the training program each year?"

"That depends on the number of vacancies we anticipate to occur in 5 years from that time. We have a model. We can predict how many surgeons would retire or downsize their practice. And we control the numbers accordingly."

"I see. So you prevent doctor unemployment. Very noble concept indeed." It was hard to read Theta's mind. But he was effusive in his praise of the Federation.

"Yes we make sure that every trainee has a job waiting for him or her when he or she finishes."

"Is that what you mean by advocating for vascular surgeons?"

"Not only that. When vascular surgeons started doing angiograms we made representations to the government to make sure we got paid on an equal footing to the radiologists. The same applies for vascular ultrasound. There was a time when vascular ultrasound was controlled by radiologists. But by up skilling ourselves and making sure the politicians are on our side, we have made sure the vascular surgeons have a right to operate an ultrasound service, and sign off on the reports."

"Indeed, the vascular surgeons have to thank your Federation and you for making sure they bring bread to the table!"

"Yes without being seen as boastful, I can proudly say that our efforts resulted in more than tripling the income of the average vascular surgeon."

"So every vascular surgeon is indebted to you!"

"Yes sir. They need to be aware of our contribution to their income."

"Very impressive Dr Alpha. Let us move to your role as head of the department of vascular surgery at Little Smoke."

"Yes I am ready to answer questions."

"Ok Dr Alpha. How would you describe your functions in this role please."

"My role is to give leadership. To provide a vision. And to make a roster."

"Is it true that you did not talk to Dr Beta for many years?"

"We had our misunderstandings. But we have resolved them now."

"Who else is in the department?" Everybody knew that the seemingly glowing testimony to Alpha and the Vascular Federation that Theta was building up was a prelude to something. Now it was becoming clearer what his strategy was going to be. It was like the roller coaster notching up and up in a slow gentle ascent. All riders knew that a precipitous fall was coming soon. When and how was upto Theta.

"There is another doctor." He stopped short of saying the name.

"He happens to share the same surname. Is he related by any chance."

Alpha knew where this was going. He was ready.

"I stood aside from the appointments committee. They chose the best person for the job. That he happens to be my son is not my fault."

"Yes you stood out from that committee. But did you not brief them on what the needs of the departments are? Did you not tell them what your vision for the department is? I am not talking about the vision for your private practice. I am talking about the vision for the department. It is a public service appointment. The people have placed their sacred trust on you to lead the department; to give them the direction. And your son is selected for the position that Dr Lambda was in, previously. Your son lives in Big Smoke. He works there; he participates in the on-call roster there; you are covering his on calls when he is supposed to be on call at Little Smoke. You don't go to No Smoke. And you replaced a person who had his office next to No Smoke with your son. Your son lives in Big Smoke and has his office inside yours at Little Smoke. So, on many days there is no vascular cover at No Smoke. Is that the vision you had for the department? Is that the directions you gave the appointments committee?"

Here was the fall. But Alpha wasn't going anywhere without a fight.

"I object to the repeated use of the term my son!" Though shaken he was still a proud man.

"Well I am not inventing anything. I am only using the phrase you used, in your correspondence with Dr Lambda and with the medical director. You had repeatedly used 'my son' in your endeavors to coerce and cajole Lambda into leaving for 'further training'. It is also the phrase you used when you asked the medical director not to consider Dr Lambda for employment when he returned from overseas."

He submitted a series of emails which were self explanatory, and which documented how Lambda was duped into leaving only for Alpha's son to be installed in his position.

Before the court adjourned to consider these emails Mr. Theta fired a few more darts for Alpha. "The Guild of Surgeons has recommended several competencies. Indeed Lambda was supposed to have been assessed against these competencies in the ostensible "review" of his practice. Medical knowledge, technical ability and clinical judgment are only three of them. The rest apply to teamwork, cooperation, communication, professionalism and so on. Do you think you possess all these competencies?"

The recess began with these questions hanging in the air. Though Gamma smiled at him she was busy taking phone calls for which she had to leave the room. Gamma had been very happy with the way things progressed. But she was still trying to multitask as was wont of a news person.

When the court reconvened after a break, Alpha was called to the witness box again.

Mr. Theta tabled the complaint document that Alpha lodged. "Do you recognize this?" he asked him. "Do you want to refresh your memory?"

"No! I know what I wrote," said Alpha.

"Fair enough. I am not going to cast aspersions on your memory like you did of Lambda's memory. Even though you are 12 years older than him you questioned if he had dementia!"

"I was upset that he violated the principles of vascular surgery at many levels."

"That was your belief. We will let the experts testify and decide if you were right or wrong. But there is a code of conduct for medical practitioners. Here is a list of violations in that document. You have vilified and name called this man left right and center. Even if he is a murderer you have no business to use these terms."

Alpha was silent. He was looking down at the carpet.

"And, Dr Alpha, you have called Dr Lambda dishonest. In your rant you had said that his problem was not lack of skills or judgment. It was dishonesty. Do you stand by that statement now?"

Again Alpha did not answer.

"Ok Dr Alpha are you an honest man?"

The opposition lawyer jumped to his feet. "Objections your honor! We don't need to attack the personal virtues of my client on the pretext of cross examination."

"I am coming to the point, your honor. I just want a yes or no answer!"

"You may proceed!" said the chief judge.

"Yes" said Alpha. There was no conviction in his voice.

"You said in your complaint that Dr Lambda was a dishonest man. You said that this was his problem; that he cannot be rehabilitated. Correct?"

"Yes."

You also said that his problem was not technical deficiency or any other correctable defect. It was plain dishonesty! Correct?"

"Yes."

"You are a senior examiner; you are the head of the department. And you say that his problem is not technical."

"I thought he was dishonest." There was no force in his voice.

"So if we can prove that he was not dishonest, he should be perfectly fine to practise surgery?"

Alpha was silent. Theta went further. "I take it as a yes. Am I correct?"

Alpha nodded.

"Then why, may I ask, did you send him for 'further training'?"

This was the coup de grace. Alpha was silent, unable to justify his own actions. The usually articulate and authoritative man was now silent, looking at the carpet, wishing that the ground would open up and swallow him.

"So doctor you conducted your own investigations and conveyed your findings about this case to the Medical Board. You are a senior surgeon and president of the Federation. So when you conduct an investigation, people will take note of your findings. You have a responsibility to be fair and neutral!"

"I was very fair."

"You don't seem to have an insight into your conduct yet. Let me draw your attention to the complaint that Lambda made regarding the appointment of your son to his position. If you are conducting an investigation against Lambda don't you think you should have declared this glaring conflict of interest up front?"

Again he was met with silence.

Theta continued. He had to twist the knife deeper, now that he had his opponent down and out.

"When you conduct an investigation there is a principle called the principle of natural justice. It is also called right of reply. Did you give Lambda a right of reply before coming to your convoluted conclusions?"

"We have not spoken for more than a year."

"That was your choice not to speak to Dr Lambda. You were avoiding him after cheating him out of his job and replacing him with your son."

Again, Alpha was silent.

"In fact Lambda tried to call you and email you. You did not answer."

"I was busy."

"I can understand that you are a busy man. But you are making conclusions about a doctor. You are using your high standing in society to undermine another doctor. Don't you think it is imperative that you give him natural justice."

"There was no malice in my actions." Alpha knew that if a malicious motive could be proven he could be sued for defamation.

"No malice! My foot! In my many decades of legal practice I am yet to encounter a complaint that is so offensive and bereft of any human decency!"

Now that he had his man on the brink he had to drive home his advantage. He knew the judges were listening. He had their ear. If he could discredit Dr Alpha and show them what kind of a man he was, anything he said would not hold water. This was part of his multipronged strategy.

Alpha left, fully deflated. Down but not out, thought Theta. He needed to throw the kitchen sink at this man. Otherwise he would make a come back.

Next up was Dr Vector, summoned by Lambda's legal team. First they went through his qualifications and experience. He was head of the department in a suburban hospital at Big Smoke. He was middle aged, moderately experienced and nondescript otherwise. He was not one of the stars of the profession. Nor was he professorial material. But he had been nominated by the Vascular Federation for the Medical Board. He was puzzled why he was subpoenaed. The cross examination began in earnest.

"Dr Lambda applied for a job at your hospital a few weeks prior to the complaint that led to his suspension. He was shortlisted and interviewed. But he did not get the job. In fact the vacancy was not filled on that occasion. No one got the job."

"Yes Sir."

"Why was he and other candidates shortlisted and interviewed, when you did not plan on selecting anyone?"

"That is not true. We did make a selection but the candidate did not pass the references."

"Yes we know. Here is the report of the appointments committee. It says you had recommended that he not be appointed, and that he had a complaint to the Medical Board coming up against him soon. On what basis did you make this recommendation?" Mr. Theta tabled a report that he had obtained under right to know rules.

"His previous colleagues were not supportive."

"Who exactly were these previous colleague or colleagues, may we know?"

"Dr Alpha was his previous head of the department."

"Yes we know that. But the candidate did not name Dr Alpha as one of his referees."

Dr Vector gathered his thoughts. He said "Dr Alpha is so well known in the country. If a candidate had worked in Little Smoke in vascular surgery it was imperative upon us that we rang him, whether he was named as a referee or not."

"Fair enough. I laud you for being diligent. So when you called him, what was the feedback from Dr Alpha?"

"He was very negative about the candidate, and..."

"And what Dr Vector?" asked Theta, honing in on a point, leading his prey towards the trap.

"He said there was a major complaint he was about to lodge. He said that in his opinion Dr Lambda's licence should be revoked."

"Did he tell you details about the complaint?"

"He outlined the issues, if I remember correctly."

"And you took him at his word?"

"He is well respected. I will be a fool to ignore his opinion."

"I agree with you. If I were in your position I would have taken it seriously too." For the first time Mr. Theta seemed to be in agreement with his quarry.

He continued "In six weeks time you were in the Medical Board panel hearing the very same complaint that he was alluding to. Don't you think it would have compromised your position as a judge, when you had prior knowledge of the complaint from the complainant's mouth?"

"I was not sure." Dr Vector was on the defensive.

"If you were not sure, did you at least declare this to anyone? You were one of two people in the panel. You were the only vascular surgeon in the panel. Don't you think it would have been better for you to step aside and let someone else hear the case?"

"In retrospect, yes" Was it a surrender or admission? But Theta was not done yet.

"You were recommended to the Medical Board by the Vascular Federation, weren't you?"

"Yes periodically the Federation recommends a few names to be on Medical Board hearings. Usually the minister accepts the recommendations as we are the controlling body of the specialty in the country."

"So here's the deal. You were appointed based on the recommendation by the Federation; the Federation also looks after your financial interests by protecting the rights to do angiograms, ultrasound and so on; it even fights to increase reimbursements for key codes in the medical benefits schedule. In other words you have pecuniary gain due to being a member of this Federation. You have a vested interest in the continued survival of the Vascular Federation as a powerful lobbying body to enhance your earnings. And you are hearing a complaint made by the president of the Federation the existence of which is important for augmenting your financial position. Can't you see the conflict of interest?"

"I did not see it that way at that time."

"Do you see it at least now?"

"Yes sir!" was the short answer as Dr Vector shuffled uncomfortably in his seat.

"At the very least you should have declared your conflict of interest up front. You did not do so because you never expected to be challenged, did you?"

Dr Vector was silent.

"Do you communicate with Dr Alpha regularly?" asked Mr. Theta, pushing further.

"Yes we do talk about matters related to the Federation."

"How do you communicate?"

"We meet at journal clubs; we call each other if necessary; and..."

"And what?"

"Sometimes we text each other."

"I thought texting is only for teen agers," a smiling Theta said as the judges laughed. A rare light moment in the courtroom. Such occurrences needed to be savored.

He tabled a document, showing it to Dr Vector.

"This is a copy of a series of text messages between Dr Alpha and Dr Vector." The witness's face ashened as he saw the contents.

"I will read it for your benefit your honors," as he held the piece of paper in his right hand, like an AK 47. Knowledge is power they say. At that point the knowledge of a secret conversation between two individuals was more powerful than any gun invented by man.

"Ok here we go. At 5.45 pm on the day before the hearing Dr Vector gets a text from Dr Alpha. "Have you banned him yet?"

There was a stunned silence in the room.

Theta continued, "At 6.15 pm you replied "Tomorrow."

"I meant the hearing was for tomorrow."

"I understand that as you were going to ban him tomorrow."

At this point the Medical Board lawyer intervened. "Please your honors. Don't allow the lawyer to ascribe motives to my client."

But the motive was a moot point. The main issue was that there had been contact between the complainant and the adjudicator. The judges were not impressed.

Mr. Theta continued "On the next day, the day of the hearing, at 11 o'clock you get a text saying "How is it going?"

"That was before the hearing."

"No! The Medical Board recordings clearly state that the hearing started at 10.15 am. You received this text while you were hearing this case."

"He may have sent it at 11 o'clock. But that doesn't mean that I looked at it."

"No. We have the whole transcript from your service provider. You received the text at 11.00'24. You checked it at 11.02'09. The hearing went on till 12.15 before they adjourned for lunch."

Dr Vector was silent for a moment. Then he said "I was on call for my hospital. So I had my phone on me in silent mode." The voice was feeble. He had been found out. The electronic media of the present day is the closest to thing to God that man has ever invented. It was like thought crime. Put your thoughts out in cyber space and you will never know when it will come back to bite you. The same for the ubiquitous CCTV. No one can do anything without being caught, with evidence, at some point in the future. Now Dr Vector was facing his day of reckoning.

"And you reply, at 12.16 pm, that is as soon as you break up for lunch, 'Almost there.' What did you mean by that doctor?"

"I meant that the hearing was almost over."

"Wow! You still deny that you aided and abetted in this crime!" Now Theta's voice was stern. The objection to the use of the word crime was over ruled by the panel. They were appalled by what had gone on.

"He replied at 12.17'01 'I want the fucker out of my region before the end of the day!' And you checked this message at 12.17'34. You replied at 12.34 '01 Aye aye captain.'

Dr Vector kept looking at the ground.

Theta pressed on. At 3.20 pm, and we know that the proceedings were over by 3.12 pm, you texted Dr Alpha 'Mission accomplished.' And he replied 'Thank you so much. Shall meet at the conference in two weeks. We should go out and have a meal on this.' There are other conversations that show how close you are with Dr Alpha. In fact he was grooming you as one of the budding stars of the Federation. You were right under his spell. Thank you for coming. I am done with my questioning."

The case was taking an entirely unexpected turn. What started as a case to restore the licence of a banned surgeon was rapidly spewing out so many sub plots that it would be hard for the judges to get their heads around the whole picture. It would appear that they had stumbled upon a web of corruption and nepotism, much of which could be criminal activity. What do they do now? Do they just turn a blind eye to this cartel-like behavior of a group of surgeons and just concentrate on the case before them? Do they ignore the instances where medical records had been criminally tampered with and just worry about Dr Lambda's licence? If Dr Vector had been in illegal contact with the complainant before during and after the hearing that would bring into question the status of the very hearing that resulted in the ban on Dr Lambda. Really this hearing had opened up the Pandora's Box, literally.

They adjourned for lunch. There was one more witness, this time on behalf of Lambda, and then Dr Lambda himself was to give evidence. That would be the end of this harrowing ordeal.

Chapter 20

They were seated at the canteen of the court complex. There were many courthouses and there were plaintiffs, defendants and their legal teams, support persons and of course the police. Though these courts did not hear criminal cases they were still potential flashpoints for opposing parties to turn violent. Therefore police, security guards and bailiffs were everywhere. This was the place also where the country's best barristers pitted their wits and debating skills against each other. And there were many sub plots to each case with interested parties ranging far beyond just the disputants.

The atmosphere in the canteen was tense but there was laughter on and off. As is human nature, however grave the situation was, man cannot refrain from smiling or laughing periodically. Mr. Theta had said the lunch was on him. Only Mr. Theta, his assistant, a young aspiring lawyer in her late twenties, and Gamma were present besides Lambda.

He was munching away at his Cesar salad as he looked into Gamma's eyes. "You are looking great!" he said, and added "I thought you had abandoned me," with a genuine hurt in his voice.

"Abandoned you? Nothing can be further from the truth. Gamma and her team of sleuths delivered us all the vital pieces of information we used. We used so much ammunition the whole court house was on fire!" Mr. Theta was very pleased with the way things had gone in the two days so far.

"This is the best case I have done in my career! And I have had a few high profile successes. I mean what I say when I say this is the best. Thanks to Gamma we attacked them left right and center."

Gamma blushed. "My contribution was miniscule. It was your style of delivery and choice of words and timing that slam dunked them. Also what was done to Lambda was a criminal injustice. So it was easy to pick holes in their arguments."

Lambda told them about the train incident in the morning. "I thought it was a very bad omen and augured for a bad day in court. But the moment I saw you in the gallery I knew it was going to be my day."

"We have left the best for the last. The next witness coming up will be the icing, thanks to Gamma," said Mr. Theta, looking gratefully at Gamma.

"You could have called me, or answered my calls. What you did was exactly what Alpha did to me after he usurped me with his son," he said looking at her with a genuinely hurt expression.

"Oh you poor baby. I will make it up to you. I did not want to distract you. I thought it is best that you stayed focused. In any case all is well that ends well."

"Will it end well?" asked Lambda. "Who is the next witness that you are making a big thing about? Beta? Has he turned coat again?"

"These things are difficult to predict. I think we are winning. But it will take them many weeks or months to write their judgment. You just have to wait. As for the next witness, it is a surprise. You will see when you see." Mr. Theta warned him about the notoriously slow pace at which the legal system works. "They have to be extremely careful. They have to consider every bit of information and make a very thorough and thoughtful decision. They have to consider other side issues that we have raised. So patience is what is necessary."

The court convened again after lunch. Everyone was weary and tired by now. They wanted the proceedings to be over soon. The whole process had been draining for all present, except perhaps for Lambda's medical experts who were doing a victory lap with smiles, hand shakes and bows all around. They were even nice to the Board's medical expert. They were the ultimate professionals, who could switch on and off their fangs at will. But for all others including the judges this had been exhausting. Not only did they have to go through medical details they had also had to listen to the personal dramas, injustices and potentially criminal activities. They wanted the hearing to be over so they could get their heads around what had just transpired, and then form opinions.

The next and penultimate witness was ushered in. This was the last person to give evidence before Lambda was called up to answer some final questions. There was silence in the room as the bailiffs ushered in the witness. He was a balding man in black suit, and a bow tie. Yes it was the Director of Standards of the Guild of Surgeons! Lambda had to do a double take! This was the man who was the kingpin in the cartel that the Guild of Surgeons had become! Why was he here? Was he going to screw him up here too? He was the man who organized the so called review on his practice. He was the man who kept changing the terms of reference like changing one's clothes, or rather a snake shedding old skin. As far as Lambda was concerned he was the father of all evil, even more than Alpha himself. This was the man who unceremoniously booted Lambda out of his office.

He was introduced as the Director of Standards; he quickly corrected "ex director!" This was a surprise. Lambda had known this man to be a survivor. He was like a Tuatara. He survived many restructurings; he was in the forefront of driving vascular surgery as a separate specialty from general surgery; he was in some position of power or other for decades. Finally he had become an employee of the Guild. Lambda had thought he would not see the back of this man during his career. Unfortunately for Lambda he was not an insider of this powerbroker's clique. Therefore he was left out in the cold. He realized now what might have been, had he ingratiated himself to this man prior to Alpha's assault on his career. He may not have survived, as Alpha would have brought his son in, come what may; but he may have had a softer fall. And made a living somewhere else.

"I resigned yesterday," began the apparatchik.

Lambda couldn't believe his ears. This man was almost like the office furniture at the Guild. He was always there in one capacity or another. And now he is gone? It was like the sun had set on the East and there was peace on earth again. Such was the magnitude of this change.

The man did look the part of a surgeon. He was suave and silken in his gestures, and spoke softly. It was no wonder why everyone was friendly with him. A friend to all is a friend to none said Aristotle. Whose friend was this man? His smiling face belied an iron will and an inexorable ambition. Why was he there? Surely he had done enough damage already.

Thank you for attending, started Mr. Theta, as he guided the witness. Lambda was surprised that Dr Bowtie had attended the trial as a witness for him. Yes indeed Gamma had lived up to her word when she said there was a major surprise awaiting him. But how did she know what was coming? He was puzzled.

"I am here to rectify some matters that have arisen under my watch," he began. "When vascular surgery separated as a different specialty few of us got together and formed the Federation. After some time we managed to wriggle out of the control of the Guild. That gave us the strength of being part of a larger group, the Guild of Surgeons, and at the same time the power to control what happened within this new specialty."

"We had unmitigated power to select trainees, train them, conduct exam, and regulate them. It resulted in a lot of good things, but at the same time, as you know, absolute power corrupts absolutely."

"There is an unusually high number of children of vascular surgeons who are also vascular surgeons. They are all good surgeons. But it is about the opportunity. Most doctors with the drive and dedication can be trained to be surgeons. But there needed to be a separator that would help select a few out of many who apply. We needed to control the selections. We devised many methods but all of them are prone to manipulation by those in the know. So it was inevitable that the children did well."

"But in the case of most of us, once the offspring gets the opportunity they are left to make their own future. But not so in the case of Dr Alpha. He is a control freak and wanted to micromanage every step of his son's career."

"Also we have the problem of overseas graduates. It is really a nuisance. The Federation, and by proxy the Guild, tightly controls the numbers. But the government allows doctors to emigrate to our country, much to our chagrin. So we needed to protect our interests without being seen as being a Mafia or cartel. We had to let them integrate into the system."

"If we just closed our eyes the problem wouldn't go away. So we engaged these doctors and devised various schemes which would help them become part of the work force. But these were in reality obstacles. True, we ensured that standards were maintained but in the case of many experienced doctors these procedures just took away many years of practice when they were at the peak of their careers. Many were pushed to go to remote areas. Others were used as stop gap personnel till our own trainees were ready."

"Because of my interpersonal skills and negotiating abilities I found myself in the thick of all these developments. While it was thrilling and exciting to be part of an elite group, it was doing a lot of harm to me as a person. I couldn't begin to imagine how I had changed from an idealistic romantic who was in the profession to help patients, to a mean power broker who trampled on others to get what I wanted."

"That is the reason I quit."

There was total silence for a few minutes. It was like everyone had witnessed a confessional. It was inspiring to see the change in this man.

"So what was your involvement in this case?" asked the chief judge.

"Dr Alpha wanted me to arrange a review of Dr Lambda's practice. The remit was to suggest Dr Lambda go away for a period of time for further training. I swear by god I did not know anything about Dr Lambda's position being given to Alpha's son. So we organized two surgeons to do this review. And I personally made sure that the terms of reference and the report were changed as many times as necessary to achieve what we set out to achieve."

"But it was a draft report, not a completed report; and it contained many errors," Mr. Theta objected.

"The main thing was that there was a report in writing. Then it was up to Alpha to use it in the way he wanted. If the motive was to really improve Lambda's performance he could have done that. If the motive was to get rid of Lambda at the time of his choosing, that could also be done."

"But isn't the Guild of Surgeons liable legally?" asked the judge.

"Our role is to make sure that the reviewers were suitably qualified. The review was neither commissioned by the Guild, nor conducted by the Guild. So we are not responsible for what the hospital did with the report."

"Well that is like having the cake and eating it. The Medical Board still refers to it as the Guild of Surgeons' review. It confers it an official status and a respect that it would not normally attach to a report by the hospital," said a panel member.

"Exactly. That is the duplicity that we created. That is why I got sick of it all."

"Thank you Dr Bow tie for being frank and honest with us. You may go now."

That brought an end to all other proceedings. The final stage was set to question Dr Lambda one last time, and give him an opportunity to say anything else that may have popped up during the trials.

"Dr Lambda have you got anything else to say in your defense?" asked the chief of the panel.

"Truth shall set you free," said Lambda.

"We are all trying to work out what the truth is. But do you have anything to add to what has already been placed before us?" he asked.

"No your honor. I trust you will do what is righteous," said Lambda looking directly into his eyes.

"Of course that is our mission. But there is a law of the land. We need to respect that," said the arbitrator. He continued, "In the absence of further submissions I will summarize what we have heard so far."

He went on to briefly summarize the evidence on both sides.

"It will take us time for us to review, understand and come to conclusions about the proceedings. But in the mean time I need to know about your current practice."

"You have banned me from practicing medicine. Now you are asking about current practice. The answer is nil; zero; zilch. How can you prohibit someone from getting into water and yet demonstrate that they can swim?" shot back Lambda dejectedly.

In fact he was asked to fill a form by the Medical Board prior to the proceedings. There he was asked about work since last meeting. He left it blank. And the clerk who collected the papers joked "We would be worried if this section was populated." What a macabre sense of humor? It was like telling the relatives of some one who had been murdered, "We would be worried if the corpse was breathing." He had to smile wryly at the insensitive remark.

"We are concerned about the safety of our patients. Whatever your individual circumstances may be, and whatever the rights and wrongs of the accusations are, patient safety is paramount. When you haven't worked for several months we need to be satisfied that your skills are still intact," the judge said in a stern voice.

"Don't people take time out to travel and return to their jobs after several months? Don't the trainees be allowed to work independently after they complete training, based on the final exam? How is my situation different your honor?"

"We understand what you are saying. But we have to go by the protocols. Also, remember, the law is inflexible. When you challenge conditions imposed by the Medical Board in a court of law, the court can modify the conditions. But when you challenge a total ban, we are allowed to either lift the ban or leave it in place."

We are not allowed to impose new conditions. That is the problem we have, unless the law is changed. But you won't benefit from any future law changes." There was a hint of sadness in the judge's voice. His hands were tied.

It was all very clear now to Lambda. The modus operandi of people like Alpha was to put their enemies on this hamster wheel. They would never be able to get off the wheel anytime soon. They will rot in purgatory. The complaints need not be true. The doctor may be innocent. But those who were savvy with the system were using complaints as an instrument of bullying. And for all the sanctimonious pronouncements against bullying in surgery no one wanted to fix the problem. There was neither popular sentiment nor political will that would effect change.

Chapter 21

"**W**e have a lot to catch up on," said Gamma as they were leaving the court complex. "Why don't you have dinner with me. You can come to my apartment but I have to tell you upfront I am not in any mood for sex."

"Neither am I. I just want to hold hands and talk."

"That makes it two of us. Let's meet at seven," she said as she went over to Theta and his team to congratulate them and to say good bye.

He went back to Little Smoke and had a shower. Then he was back on the roads getting back to Big Smoke. It was a long round trip. But he did not mind. Driving kept his mind occupied, and his thoughts away from the unpleasant happenings of the recent past.

"You did well. I was proud of you," said Gamma as she gave him a peck on his cheek while accepting the roses.

"But the judge was a wet blanket. His last statement has killed all positive thoughts I had about this process."

"They have to say that in order not to raise your expectations. You are innocent. And they have to do what is fair by you."

"I am not holding my breath. Every institution that I have come across in the past few years has acted with bias. There is institutionalized bias in this place. "

"Hey it is not bad. We are good people. The goodness of human nature will trump the greed and hatred of the few you have encountered recently. I know about the chief of the panel. He is known to have given out fair decisions consistently."

"Ok let's leave that and talk about us," said Lambda, as he hugged her again. I have missed you a lot. Where were you in the dire hours of need of my life? How I missed you!"

Gamma looked at him with loving eyes. "I did not want to distract you. I was dealing with problems of my own!"

"What?" he said. But in his heart of hearts he knew what it was. Yes it must be the breast lump! He always had a fear this was going to turn out nasty. He feared the worst. Why is god so heartless? The only person who is helping me unconditionally is struck down with disease. What did I do to deserve this?

"You would have guessed it by now. Yes it is the breast lump. I had to have surgery. But it is not that bad. Things will be alright." Though there was fear in her eyes she tried to put on a bold face. It is a cancer alright. Don't worry. It is out."

It was as though someone had given him a blow on his head. Though he knew what it was going to be, he was hoping against hope that it would be benign. Once hope is gone, life becomes unbearable, at least in the short run.

"I was worried about you. That's why I called you many times. But you never answered."

"I know; three hundred calls; forty two voice messages; thirty texts and twenty two emails'," she smiled. "I know how much you care for me. But if I had answered, I would have distracted you from your work. You needed to be focused on undoing the injustice done to you. Besides, both of us would have gone on an emotional bender. That would have weakened my resolve to fight the bastard too," she said.

She said "It was like someone saving her virginity for the wedding night. Every time you called I would almost answer, and then stop myself. I was waiting for the grand reunion at your trial. I was getting a thrill out of denying myself. I felt an exhilaration each time I did not answer your call, thinking that it would make the happiness that much greater when we eventually met. And it was worth the wait!"

She continued "I had a wide excision and radiotherapy. I have completed that. The decision about chemo will be made next week. Though I did not answer your calls, every time you tried to contact me I received a boost. I kept a count because I felt loved. Also the fact that you tried to call even on the day before your trial meant a lot to me. Your love and care helped me to get through radiotherapy."

"I am sorry I wasn't with you to encourage you and support you!" he said guiltily.

"No my sister was there to give physical support. Your efforts to contact me gave me moral support" she said, finishing off the salad. "You won't believe how many times I felt like quitting. But I thought I needed to be there till your case was heard at least! So I hardened my resolve to fight back."

"We are both fighting existential threats," he smiled wryly.

"I grilled some salmon for you. You like salmon don't you."

"I love salmon."

"See. I do remember," she said as she cleared the table. He helped her to load the dishwasher while she took the salmon out of the oven.

"Smells delicious!" he exclaimed.

"I marinated overnight. I know you like a bit of spice."

"Yummy!" he said tasting a small piece even as she laid out the table.

"Hold it till I organize everything! Would you like to have some wine?"

"The usual red please," he said as he tried to help her with her tasks. Not that she needed help but the fact that he was trying to help meant a lot to her.

"How did you know Dr Bow tie was coming to give evidence?" he asked her. "It was a total surprise to me. He was the arrogant sod who threw me out of his office!" he said.

"I guessed that was the man. It was not planned you know. When I went to this ceremony proclaiming the end of bullying for eons, this guy was trying to hit on me. I realized from his talk that he was your villain. But I must confess the power and atmosphere in that place is intoxicating. No wonder a lot of young women with starry eyes fall prey. Will you get mad if I say he almost succeeded in seducing me?"

"Come on! We are not in a relationship yet. I don't own you. How can I get angry even if you had slept with him?"

"I almost did! But something in me woke up suddenly when he showed his total disregard for patients. I stopped him. Also I had switched on my recorder at the start. You know the journalist in me will never leave me!"

"Fucking woman! Are you taping me too?" he asked in mock anger.

"With you it is different. There I attended a ceremony and it was partly work related. Here it is home!" she hugged him and they started a lip lock and tongue play which lasted several minutes. Neither wanted to part.

"Ok big boy! I don't feel like full sex for now. I need to get over my health issues'" she said, finally separating from him. "Let's eat."

She explained how, after he groped her, she stopped him, and threatened to expose him. That would have been the end of a carefully groomed, painstakingly maintained legendary name. Dr Bow tie soon played ball. He agreed to tow her line.

" 'I can't go public in helping Lambda while I am still a part of our organization,' he said. I told him he should resign his position. He was close to retirement anyway. He weighed his options and came round quickly. It was he who gave me information about the nurse and helped me extract a confession."

"So you did not abandon me!" he said.

"Not at all. I was working on this project. I mean you are my project. That gave me something to do that would take my mind away from this bloody cancer."

"So Theta isn't as brilliant as I thought he was?"

"Well, my team helped him. We worked hard in the back ground. We provided him with all the ammunition. But he was the one who directed the fire. You should give credit to him too."

They talked about all the things they had missed in each other's lives. He left just before midnight.

"I think it will take several weeks for them to deliver the judgment. Let's have our fingers crossed." She said as they bade good bye.

Chapter 22

"**I** am at the harbor bridge," read the text. Gamma did a double take. Why is Lambda trying to text her when she was at the doctor's office.

"Why are you there," she replied. Just then she was ushered into the doctor's office. She switched off her phone. This was an important consultation. She could not afford to have the distractions of her mobile phone.

The consultation took about an hour. The doctor went through the pros and cons of chemotherapy. His recommendation was that Gamma should have it. It was a big decision. She had to consider the implications for her job as well as personal health. Was the small percentage gain in life expectancy worth it? Would it not be easier to trust her luck and take her chances? But her luck had not been great in the past. And she thought of Lambda. Though they were not in a relationship he was one person she really cared for and who she knew would want her to live for as long as possible.

Having thought about it again and again she still couldn't decide. Then the thought came to her mind 'why not ask Lambda?' Perhaps he could give her a better insight. She remembered his message. 'The bugger must be enjoying his climb! Should I call him now? He may not be able to talk to me because of high winds and background noises. And the signal may not be good.'

Then she thought about Lambda perched on top of the bridge, trying to fish out his mobile phone from the pockets scrambling to answer the call before it stopped ringing. What if he let go, or lost his balance? A sudden chill went through her spine. A fall from that height would kill him on the spot wouldn't it? Or leave him with broken bones or head injury. What about a spinal injury?

Just then the mobile came on. It showed ten unread messages, all from Lambda. 'Naughty boy! He shouldn't be texting from the bridge!' she thought. 'It was risky.'

She started reading the messages. Little did she know that this was going to be the worst day in her life. The day had started with her being told that she needed chemotherapy. Could it get any worse? Apparently it could!

"I have decided to end it all" it began. Tears started rolling down Gamma's cheeks. She was already at the end of her tether with the news about her chemo. How many hits could one take? The last several months had been up and down for her. And now the two setbacks in one day, before the mind's defenses could kick in.

"I did not come to this conclusion in haste. I have thought long and hard, just as I would think about a clinical problem. My career is in tatters, though I am innocent. The system in this country is such that any doctor who is accused of anything is presumed guilty until proven otherwise. The system is very slow. Once someone is put into this slow burn their careers are irreparably damaged, leave alone the emotional toll it takes on the doctors and families."

"Those who know how to play the system have entrenched themselves in the higher echelons of power. They sustain their position by undermining others and destroying potential competition by the mechanism of complaints."

"Patient safety is the slogan with which all this undemocratic empire building is done. But the patient is the last thing in their minds. A whole industry has grown out of medical defense. This is money that should be spent for patient care. But instead it is feeding and fattening a whole lot of pen pushers."

"In my case, my career is gone. The career that I built with sacrifices and hardship has been blown to smithereens by this unfair means. Even if the judge finds me innocent of the crimes that I was accused of, the Medical Board is going to say I have to work under supervision and would impose a thousand and one conditions. With the hostile colleagues in Little Smoke all out to knife me again, I will never be able to practice there again. My patients have left. My referral doctors have been turned away. My office is closed. I cannot start from scratch and survive in private practice alone. And my name has been sullied in the whole region so that getting another job will be nigh impossible."

"When Alpha did this injustice to me no one lifted a finger to help me. Everyone knew what was happening but no one opened their mouth. There is a culture of acquiescence. The medical regulators aided and abetted in this murder of my career. There is institutionalized bias."

"My life is precious. I thought of other things that I could do to be useful to this world. But I have done medicine and vascular surgery for so long that I have no skills in any other profession or activity. I cannot reinvent myself into someone else. And sitting at home as a depressed person is not something I could ever contemplate. I have never been a burden to others and I do not intend to change that."

"So how useful is my life? It is useless in its current state. It is a total void. Useless to me and useless to others. The only way I can be useful is to die a high profile death. I am dying at the harbor bridge at the peak hour. Let the traffic stall for a moment and let the motorists think of the problem while they wait. Yes I had a badly tarnished and notorious life. At least let me have an honorable end. Let this increase the awareness of this hidden scourge of bullying by complaints. In my death let others live. Let the government and the regulators be moved enough to end this cancer from our medical fraternity."

"I am sorry I am doing this to you Gamma. I love you with all my heart. I will love you till my last breath, which won't be far away. You are the only person who loved and supported me unconditionally in the last few months. But I don't see a future for us together. You don't want to live with a painted and tainted surgeon for the rest of your life. You have a stellar career ahead of you. Your health problems are temporary and you will overcome them with your will power. If there is another birth let us meet, perhaps earlier in our lives."

"I ask you one favor. If, by virtue of your position in the news industry you can raise awareness of this problem, please do so."

"As for now, good bye my darling."

Gamma was momentarily paralyzed by this loss. But she soon sprang into action. She called her media organization and the police. Send a helicopter, send boats and send the divers. Get him before he dies. Get the ambulance crews to the scene!" she screamed. She ran out of the doctor's office and got into her car in next to no time. But it was peak hour still and she just could not go as fast as she wanted to. Her mind was racing far ahead of her car. Her heart was racing as she felt the thumps in her chest. Her brain was fogged.

She had a couple of near misses as she kept changing lanes to get ahead. There was a prayer on her lips and a tear drop on her left eye. She could see helicopters circling overhead. The cancer had gone out of her mind totally. Her mind, body and soul were all craving for one thing only. He should live. But she knew, like everything else in her life lately this would also be an unfulfilled desire.

She turned on the radio. All local channels were in breaking news mode. They were at the bridge. Lambda had timed his exit well. Everyone in the city and surrounding regions knew about the suicide. Many were inconvenienced by the traffic chaos. Most were touched. A lot of people wanted to know about the Surgeons Guild's role in medicine. A few called for the minister's resignation.

She finally reached her destination. How many times had she been at the fore front with news scoops. But here she was, the news and the scoop too close to her.

A police officer recognized her, and greeted her solemnly.

"We found this at the bottom of the bridge, he said. They were a pair of loupes, the operating magnification; a head lamp; and two well worn needle holders, one the conventional type and the other Castro type.

These were the prized possessions of the painted surgeon. The tools of his trade. And he had downed his tools.

Will he achieve in death, what he couldn't achieve during his life?